"You're trembling, Natalie."

Kip's hands still molded her slender shoulders, carefully, as if he thought she might break. "What are you afraid of? Did you think I'd be brutal?"

"I'm going back inside." She couldn't control her voice, and it trembled too.

"Because you're afraid? It's really only fear of the unknown."

He pulled her completely into his arms, folding her against him, looking down at her, the lights from the house catching his fair hair, and she stiffened immediately, much too aware of the hard body close to hers. He hadn't behaved like this before and suddenly he was dangerous, as if a restraint had been lifted.

PATRICIA WILSON used to live in Yorkshire, England, but with her children all grown up, she decided to give up her teaching position there and accompany her husband on an extended trip to Spain. Their travels are providing her with plenty of inspiration for her romance writing.

If you enjoy Kip and Natalie's Madembi romance, don't miss *Forbidden Enchantment* by Patricia Wilson, Harlequin Presents #1547. Kip's sister Andrea discovers that Africa can be dangerous—particularly in the company of a man like Kane Mallory!

Books by Patricia Wilson

HARLEQUIN PRESENTS
1398—PASSIONATE ENEMY
1430—STORMY SURRENDER
1454—CURTAIN OF STARS
1469—THE GIFT OF LOVING
1518—PERILOUS REFUGE
1547—FORBIDDEN ENCHANTMENT

HARLEQUIN ROMANCE
2856—BRIDE OF DIAZ
3102—BOND OF DESTINY

PATRICIA WILSON

Jungle Enchantment

Harlequin Books

TORONTO • NEW YORK • LONDON
AMSTERDAM • PARIS • SYDNEY • HAMBURG
STOCKHOLM • ATHENS • TOKYO • MILAN
MADRID • WARSAW • BUDAPEST • AUCKLAND

Harlequin Presents first edition June 1993
ISBN 0-373-11564-4

Original hardcover edition published in 1991
by Mills & Boon Limited

JUNGLE ENCHANTMENT

CHAPTER ONE

'IT'S not every day we get approached by a government.' Jonas West looked round severely at his staff to impress them with this salient fact. 'This is a commission, not some vague enquiry. The minister of culture is keen to get the opening of the dam on film *and* it's not just a whim on his part. With the opening of the Kabala Dam, Madembi will shoot into the present century. They'll have *power*! They'll have enough power to export some to less fortunate countries and they'll be all but self-sufficient.'

Everyone listened dutifully and at the back of the room Natalie sat on the edge of the table, her lips twitching with amusement. This was the lecture her father gave each time they had a film to make. He called it 'getting people on their mettle'. He shot her a suspicious look and she straightened her face, looking back solemnly, loving the deep, gruff sound of his voice.

'This has been a huge undertaking,' he resumed. 'A vast hydro-electricity scheme that will make it possible for Madembi to use its other resources. Technology will transform the country and we're going to let the whole world see. We're going to put them on the map! We show the dam, the country, the past and the future. Hospitals will be built, schools, factories. *This* had better be good! Natalie flies out this week to do the groundwork as usual. Be ready to follow her about two weeks later. Any questions?' He snapped out the enquiry, casting a rather fierce look around, just daring them.

The result was entirely predictable. There were no questions and he nodded his grey head, dismissing them. He was a commanding figure, accustomed to taking the lead, making decisions. Jonas West had been a power in television for years before he set up his own independent production unit. He had never known what is was to be anything but successful and Westwind Productions was very successful indeed, the films they made selling all over the world.

The little meeting broke up and Natalie slid gracefully off the table to wait for a private word with her father. Ray Hanson winked at her on his way out.

'Into the breach, men! Take no prisoners!' It was only a quiet observation but his stance was indicative of his comment, the pointing finger and outstretched arm giving the game away entirely. Natalie grinned and closed the door behind them all.

'Cheeky young devil!' Jonas West glared at the closed door. 'One day, I'm going to really give him his marching orders.'

'And you'll never get such a talented cameraman again,' Natalie reminded him as she came to sit by his desk. 'You've got to admit, Dad, you lay it on thick. That's the third pep-talk this week on that particular subject.'

'Necessary.' He beetled his thick brows at her and did a bit more glaring. 'Whose side are you on anyway?'

'I have to be neutral.' She laughed up at him, tossing back her long black hair. 'Being the daughter of the boss has certain disadvantages.'

'And certain advantages,' he reminded her with a keen look. 'Just one word from you and I'll get rid of Neil Bradshaw. I'll get rid of the girl too.'

Neither of them were smiling now, and Natalie looked away from the eyes that saw every expression that crossed her face.

'We've been over this, Dad. Everyone has a right to a change of heart. With Neil it wasn't even that because we weren't engaged or anything like it. He simply fell in love with Paula, and who can blame him? She's a very nice girl. He told me straight out with no deceit whatever.'

'You're just like your mother,' Jonas West muttered. 'No thought of vindictiveness, no reprisals. You see everybody's needs but your own.'

'What did you expect? When somebody tells you he's getting engaged to the girl he loves do you turn round and shout? Am I supposed to say I'll knock him down because he doesn't love me? We were only going out together, after all.'

'For a whole damned year,' her father growled. 'Now you're stuck in the same company; they'll both be following you out to Africa, mooning about right under your nose!'

'They don't "moon about",' Natalie assured him. 'They're both hard workers, dedicated. Let it drop, Dad. I'm really not bothered.'

She got the same old suspicious look and then a great bear-hug.

'Just like your mother.' His eyes were slightly damp. 'Margaret had the same sweet nature. God! I miss her.' He straightened up and moved back to his desk. 'Take care out there. Madembi isn't Kensington. A dam can be a dangerous place.'

Natalie nodded, greatly relieved to be off the subject of Neil and Paula. If the rest of the team knew of her father's fiercely protective attitude towards her they

would treat her differently and she would hate that. She
had worked hard to get her present skills, university and
two years in a television studio being a good background for what she did now. She hadn't just walked
into this job because her father owned the company. He
might dote on her at home, want to protect her, but he
demanded the highest standards at work and she was
not in any way favoured.

'I'll take care,' she assured him, the words she uttered
every time he sent her out to some place to research and
plan. 'Now let's get down to details.'

He was back to business at once, the subject of Neil
dropped, and Natalie pulled her chair closer to his desk,
ready to work and listen. Her heartache was her own
business and if she had to face Neil and Paula Carlton
every day both here and in Africa then that was her
business too. One thing was sure—they would never
know. It was her own private nightmare and getting on
with her job was the only thing she could think of to
ease the daily pain.

In any case, there was never time to sit around here.
In spite of her looks, she was the trouble-shooter for the
whole unit. Her father planned but it was Natalie who
flew off to odd places, sometimes dangerous places. It
was Natalie who was expected to go in feet first and get
things moving. Jonas West made no concessions to her
sex. In his opinion a member of his staff was either good
or hopeless. It was a tribute to her skill that he trusted
her entirely and that the rest of the staff accepted this
was nothing to do with the fact that she was Natalie
West. She was good at her job, confident. They all knew
that.

There was the usual bustle and turmoil in the building
as she walked out of her father's office and into the main

offices that spread across one floor of the old Victorian block that housed Westwind Productions. Looking down she could see the frantic hustle of London's traffic but up here it seemed remote, the sound muted. Next week she would be in Africa, on her own, working against the clock as usual, nothing easy. It would give her a little time away from Neil, until he brought the team out. One day it would stop hurting.

'Am I fired?' Ray Hanson came into the room and she laughed, her eyes twinkling.

'Not yet. I spoke up for you.'

He held up his hands in mock-horror. 'Listen, don't do me any favours. When you and your dad start battling I don't want to be even mentioned.'

'You mean you hear our raised voices from time to time?' Natalie grinned and he nodded vigorously.

'Battle of the Titans. I expect chairs to start flying.'

'It's all words,' she assured him soothingly.

'And she's no Titan.' Neil Bradshaw came in too, his eyes on Natalie's amused face, and she felt her facial muscles stiffen with the effort to keep the smile there. She wanted to run to him and be swept up, to hear him tell her to wake up because it was a bad dream and nothing else. He could hardly do that, though, when Paula wore his ring.

He was dark, like Natalie herself, but without the startling blue-blackness of hair that made her so unusual. Everything about Neil was easygoing, warm, comfortable. As he walked forward she had to stop herself from raising her hand towards him. It was still too raw inside her for any light-hearted teasing and to give him credit he had never attempted any. He was too considerate for that, even though he didn't realise what an effort it took to face him each day.

'Watch your step out in Madembi.' He stood close to her, looking down at her beautiful face, his expression serious. 'They may have a dam but they also have plenty of jungle, wild animals and disease.'

'I always watch my step. I'm not as dainty as I look.'

It sounded a bit coy and she blushed but he took it all seriously, watching her with a sudden intensity.

'I'm aware of that. Funny, I never worried about you when we were going out together; now I'm uneasy and it's got nothing to do with me at all.'

'It never had,' Natalie said quickly. 'The boss sits right behind that door.' She nodded towards her father's office and was surprised to see Neil's face darken close to annoyance.

'Yes. I wonder how long I'll last here?'

'You're part of the team—the producer—and you just happen to have an exceptional television voice. We all double up. Where are we going to get anyone like you if you leave? Surely you're not thinking about it?'

Her anxiety seemed to please him because he smiled and relaxed.

'*I'm* not. It did occur to me though that your father might be thinking of getting rid of me. He's been giving me some black looks.'

'Well, it's nothing to do with me,' Natalie said hastily. 'We all get our share of those.'

'And you never deserve them,' he murmured. 'You battle for all of us. Ray would have had the boot already if it hadn't been for you. He can't seem to be serious for even a minute.' There was a certain amount of friction between Neil and Ray, nothing she could quite put her finger on. She used to imagine it was because she got on so well with Ray but of course it couldn't be that now that Neil was engaged to Paula.

'He's not likely to get anything of the sort,' Natalie assured him as his face set into lines of annoyance, glad that Ray had left the room for a minute. 'Dad's a businessman. He recognises the best when he sees it.'

'Maybe we all do, sooner or later,' Neil said softly, with such an obvious change of subject that she almost gasped. His hand touched her hair and then fell away quickly as Paula walked in, her short fair curls bobbing about in that way they had. She was like a happy child, deeply in love with Neil, and Natalie hadn't the heart to begrudge her the happiness. A small chill settled over her. If Neil was going to be like this then the sooner she got away the better.

'I'm so excited about going to Africa,' Paula told Natalie, not even noticing that Neil moved away as she came in.

'You'll stay in my luggage and never be allowed out,' he said, smiling at her with the look of astonishment that always came over his face when Paula appeared.

'Isn't he bossy?' she appealed to Natalie. 'When we're married I have to give up my job. What do you think of that?'

'I never interfere between engaged couples,' Natalie said smoothly. If she didn't get out soon she would burst into tears. Her eyes met Neil's and his face softened. As Paula went happily on her way he moved close to Natalie again.

'Natalie.' She never heard what he was going to say because he wasn't the only one calling her name.

'Natalie!' Her father appeared in the door of his office and she escaped gladly. She must never be close to Neil again and she knew it.

'What was he talking about?' Her father snapped out the question as she closed the door behind her.

'The forthcoming production and——'

'Natalie!' His warning growl assured her that he could still read her expression as easily as when she had been a child.

'He was wondering when he'll get the push.'

'Second sight,' he observed curtly. 'Bradshaw should go far—and fast.'

'I hope you haven't been interfering in my affairs?' Natalie enquired angrily, her face flushing with colour.

'What affairs?' He smiled like a hungry tiger. 'You only went out with him for a year, after all.'

'Remember it!' she snapped, turning to the door.

'You're fired,' he assured her laconically.

'Good. I hate it here. I'll set up a rival firm. After all, I've got every contact you have.'

His booming laugh was no surprise and she turned into his arms as he hugged her. 'Anybody hurts you, my lamb, and I'll bite them in two,' he growled, his hug almost taking her breath away. 'In case I forget later, watch your step in Madembi.'

'You've said that already.' Natalie laughed and he looked down at her sternly.

'I never repeat myself!'

'Of course you don't. No more than twice a day.'

She felt a bit more happy and when she went out Neil had had the good sense to get about his tasks. She spent the time looking through the previous week's shooting with Ray, making quite sure that her efforts for the last production were safely sealed off before she had to leave again.

A week later she was on her way, but her usual confidence was somewhat missing this time. As the plane approached Nairobi, Natalie felt the relaxing waves of relief that had been sadly lacking for the whole of the journey. There was still the landing, of course, but the flight was almost over. She was not a good air traveller although as often as not her job took her to many far-flung places of the world and flying was a necessity. She preferred it when she could work in England, a car or train her transport, but that sort of ease was rare. Her father seemed to attract work in far-away places.

This trip had taken it out of her more than usual for some reason, making her feel almost ill. It had been a long flight, most of the journey in darkness. To see the other passengers sleeping peacefully made matters worse and now her olive-tinted skin was pale from lack of sleep and that vague fear she could never quite shake off, however many times she flew.

Somebody would meet her, she knew that, some representative from the Madembi government. She hoped they had a room booked for her in a cool, quiet hotel because she felt more than jaded. A shower, a light meal and some sleep would restore her to normal, or near enough. Nothing in her life was exactly normal now, not since Neil had told her his news. She tried to put it right out of her mind but it refused to go, tiredness not helping at all.

She closed her eyes for a moment, unwillingly reliving the evening a month ago when her date with Neil had been the opportunity for him to announce his engagement to somebody else, the sweet good-natured girl who worked with them, a girl she had to see every day as she had also to face Neil.

She tried to be fair, logical. She had not been engaged to Neil herself; they had simply been going out together for more than a year. People did change their minds, meet someone else, but he had told Natalie more than once that he loved her, that one day they would marry.

She had been jilted with no ring to prove it and, whatever change of heart Neil had felt, it had not happened to her. She still loved him. He would never know. That was her shield, and the shield was always in place.

Her father would never know either, for all his suspicions. But she did not really have the calm serenity of her mother. She could only pretend calm, be aloof, cool, withdrawn. She had always lived on a good deal of nervous energy, tight as a bow-string, any small fears hidden. Neil had come into her life as she had lost her mother, and now that he too was gone a great gap yawned in front of her, nothing to fill it because, much as she loved and admired her father, he was not a shoulder to cry on. Jonas West believed in drive, power, retribution. If he knew how she really felt, he would crush Neil Bradshaw utterly and enjoy doing it.

Before she left, Neil's attitude seemed to have changed, making her feel guilty. He had taken to watching her, a thing he hadn't even done when they were going out together, and it was making things very uncomfortable. Pretty soon, Paula would notice. She was not quite the dumb blonde she seemed and Natalie didn't want her hurt as well. Life seemed to be getting too complicated to live at the moment. It was a good thing she had left London.

It was so hot outside the aircraft that Natalie felt faint. From an English autumn to the air-conditioned cabin and now to this heat was shock enough, without the tiredness and fear she had struggled with all the journey long. The bright light dazzled her, increasing an already bad headache, and she couldn't wait to get out of the sun.

In the airport buildings it was cooler but the crowds seemed to jostle her all over the place and for the first time in her travelling life she felt lost, incapable of asserting herself, her usual drive quite gone. Luckily she didn't have much luggage and it was soon collected, dragged over to a seat and safe.

She sat down and waited because there was nothing else to do. Whoever was meeting her would eventually find her. She rested her head back, closed her eyes and hoped for the best. Her head was drumming, a great throbbing pain that made her feel sick. She would give just about anything to go to bed right now and as soon as she got to her hotel she would simply sleep. Tomorrow she would feel better.

The crowds cleared but she remained still, her eyes closed, her head resting back against the seat, and the man who came in and looked round for her stood stock still for a moment as he saw her, a look of disbelief on his face.

His dark eyes made an instant catalogue of her appearance, his gaze searchingly intent, running over the whole of her slim figure from her finely-shaped head to the beautiful slender legs. Her hands rested lightly in her lap, the fingers long, elegant, the nails pale with no varnish. His jaw tightened, an angry breath leaving him slowly.

She was a mirage of black and gold, out of place in the world of tanned, confident people he was used to. For a moment he almost refused to believe what he saw, but this had to be the girl he was meeting; just about everybody else had gone. His dark brows drew together in annoyance and for a few seconds more he simply watched her, hoping he was wrong.

She seemed to be resting lightly, almost ready to take flight, her blue-black hair straight and long, parted in the middle, her oval face pale beneath an olive-tinted skin. The faint sheen of exhaustion about her had his eyes narrowing thoughtfully.

Her dress was black with bright yellow flowers across it, golden chains around her wrist and her neck. There was a delicate look about her that belied everything he had been told. The closed eyes were shaded with purple shadows, her mouth drooping like a sick child's. An exotic butterfly! Hell! She wouldn't survive in Madembi, or anywhere else by the look of her.

He felt a wave of irritation against his friend Gabriel Basoni but quickly suppressed it. Gabriel hadn't ordered this girl out here. Somebody at the TV company had thought up this bright idea and *this* was their advance party, this exhausted girl. If anyone had to take care of her he could just imagine who it would be. He damned Gabriel all over again and some nameless idiot in England.

'Miss West?'

The coolly authoritative voice had Natalie's immediate attention and her eyes came open slowly, sleep almost winning the battle. The dark eyes that watched her held a barely suppressed hostility that startled her and she struggled to sit upright, surprised to see an English face. Somehow she had expected to be met by an African, somebody from the minister's own office. She stared at him, momentarily unsettled.

'Yes. I'm Natalie West.' Long green eyes looked back at him, peculiarly changeable, unusual against her dark hair and tinted skin. With her eyes open she looked more exotic than ever and his lips tightened in spite of his efforts to be dispassionate.

'Kip Forsythe. As I was in Nairobi, I offered to meet you.'

She was used to people, dealt with them all the time, and she read his expression. He hadn't offered. She could tell that at once. He had been pressurised into it—no, charmed. This man didn't look as if he could be pressurised. He was too tough-looking, with a handsome, tanned, determined face, well-delineated lips, dark eyes. He was well over six feet tall and although she was way above average height herself he made her feel almost tiny. His hair was fair, bleached further by the sun, and the dark eyes looked her over and obviously found her wanting. He didn't like her.

It was clear that he had made his mind up about her on sight and he had a definite air of command—uncompromising. It almost panicked her. She needed help, not accusation. What would he say if she told him she felt ill? Somehow she knew. He would look after her, protect her and be damned disparaging without saying one word. He wasn't going to get the chance. And she wasn't going to feel scared and insignificant either.

She came to her feet, lightly and easily, almost seeming to float upwards.

'Thank you. I expect a hotel has been booked for me?'

'The very best, I assure you. Newly built and luxurious. The Kabala Hotel. The most spectacular that Madembi can offer.' His wry look told her he understood that she was used to only the best, that she was accustomed to being pampered, but she wasn't in any condition to do battle and his words had dismayed her.

'But—but I thought I would be staying here until tomorrow. It's been a long flight and I thought...'

'I'm flying you out immediately, Miss West.' His dark eyes looked faintly sardonic, skimming over her slight figure. 'We'll be in Madembi by this evening.'

'I see. I have to catch another plane.' Natalie tried to keep the depression out of her voice and evidently succeeded because after a swift glance at her he gave her a cool smile.

'A brief walk. The plane will almost catch you.' He picked up her luggage. 'Is this all? Two small cases and this bag? You're quite sure there isn't a large trunk somewhere.'

So he *had* got her categorised! She met his derisive eyes with a blaze of green.

'I travel a lot, Mr Forsythe. I don't burden myself with large amounts of luggage. My clothes have to be uncrushable. The bag is the only thing that needs care. It holds equipment.'

'The modern working woman.' He gave a brief appraisal to her clothes, the swinging skirt of her dress, the fashionable black sandals, his eyes narrowing in caustic amusement when she flushed softly, her hands smoothing her hair back from her face. 'You'll need more than uncrushable things if you're to go clambering around the Kabala Dam.'

'You can leave it safely to me, Mr Forsythe.' Natalie closed her lips firmly—end of conversation as far as she was concerned. If he had been anything but an uncompromisingly masculine figure she would have mentioned that she felt faint and sick. She kept it to herself. She had managed so far and she could manage to get to this hotel, even if it was another flight away. His opinion of her was written all over his face.

It was unusual for her to feel quite like this. In spite of her almost constant fear of flying, it had never made her feel actually ill before. No doubt a good night's sleep would put her right. She sincerely hoped so. She had managed never to be unwell so far away from home. Normally, she was pretty tough, competent and dedicated, hardly ever ill. It would be just her luck to have to throw herself on the mercy of this golden giant with scathing dark eyes.

She followed him out, back into the blazing sun, watching him walk with an easy, athletic assurance that was bordering on the autocratic. He was wearing white jeans, Italian by the look of them, and the black sports shirt was a stark contrast to the crisp fair hair. With his good looks and the brilliant hair against a golden tan he should have looked like some film star. He didn't though; at least, if he did then it was someone who only played tough roles.

She knew she would have to keep up her guard, the efficient, resilient look of a TV woman that had stood her in good stead for a very long time. It fooled everyone else, including her own father.

'Natalie's a tough little thing.' She had heard him say that plenty of times, pride in his voice, certain knowledge that she was a chip off the old block. She kept her inner quakings to herself, and now was a good time to keep up the act because she felt that at any moment this man was going to turn and say something crisply sardonic.

The plane was small, a light aircraft like a moth, red and white, parked in a small area that housed other private planes and Natalie looked rather anxiously for the pilot, hoping for a more fatherly figure who might just be interested in her headache.

'Here we are.' Kip Forsythe tossed her luggage up with no effort, taking extra care with the bag, and then motioned her to the steps, standing back to help. 'We'll get off right away. I'm cleared for take-off within the next few minutes.'

'You? You're flying us to Madembi.'

'I'm thinking about it, Miss West. If you could bring yourself to assist by getting in I'll see if I can manage it.'

'I—I didn't realise . . . You're a pilot?'

'You'd better hope so.' He shot her a look of exasperation mixed with sudden amusement. 'Look at it like this. You'll be sitting right next to me. If I do anything you don't like, you'll be able to point it out.'

He might think this was a time for caustic humour but Natalie didn't. She climbed on board, everything inside her tightening up more when she saw how small this plane was. A big aircraft was bad enough; this seemed so slight, as if there wasn't much to hold them in the air.

'How long will it take?' The question came out a bit huskily as he got in beside her and strapped himself in securely.

'Not too long. Transport is waiting at the other end. I'll have you in your hotel before you know it. Relax.'

She nearly burst into tears. Relax! He might be competent and he looked it, his every movement sure and efficient, but that didn't help at all. Suddenly she knew it would take a good deal of nerve ever to fly again. What would her father make of that? All at once, the vague fears were more than real. The engines roared into life and her headache increased with every rev. Yes. She was ill. What a stupid place to be at the mercy of this tough man. She could manage him better on her own two feet.

It was some consolation to know he wouldn't have to be managed. It was pretty obvious that he was doing a favour for someone, that he had just happened to be here and had been cajoled into picking her up. She would have to be extra polite and very calm, hope to get this over with as quickly as possible.

All the same, as the aircraft took off she closed her eyes tightly, even finding it difficult to open them when she knew perfectly well that they were airborne.

'You're safe. Open your eyes.'

The darkly amused voice got through to her and she forced herself to sit up straight and look assured. He was watching her intently, seeing the faint film of perspiration on her face.

'You're afraid. Why didn't you tell me? I would have been quite prepared to make the journey back by car. It would have meant an overnight stop on the way but we could have done that with little trouble.'

'I'm not afraid,' Natalie managed tightly. 'I'm simply tired. I've had a long flight and I can never sleep on a plane.'

'You like to keep a look-out in case you have to take the controls?' He glanced at her hands, tightly clenched in her lap. 'Tell the truth and shame the devil; you're terrified.'

'Yes.' Natalie looked down at her own clenched fingers and tried to uncurl them surreptitiously. 'It's something that's grown on me. I—I didn't realise until the flight out here just how bad it was getting. I *have* to fly! It's part of my job.'

He glanced sharply across at her, alerted by the catch in her voice.

'You seem to have two choices,' he said quietly. 'Get some professional help or resign.'

'I *have* managed to work that out for myself,' Natalie snapped, feeling like a case for a funny farm. 'As to resigning, I doubt if my father would hear of it. We're a tightly knit unit, everyone with a specific job. If I waltzed off I'd never hear the end of it at home.'

'Your father?' He looked slightly puzzled and she had to tell him. She could have kicked herself for blurting out the information.

'My father is Jonas West. He owns Westwind Productions.'

'Ah!' His dark brows were raised as comprehension dawned and Natalie stiffened further. As soon as anyone knew her job and her father's position, she got this 'Daddy's girl' attitude.

'What do you mean—ah? I get no favours, Mr Forsythe! I work damned hard so don't go imagining that——'

'You have a very prickly disposition, Miss West,' he informed her astringently. 'If you've got a chip on your shoulder, please don't take it out on me. I'm merely doing a favour, nothing more than a kindly bus driver. Any problems you have can be taken up with your psychiatrist later.'

Natalie closed her lips tightly at that, trying to forget her fears and her giant headache. He was pretty much as she had assessed him: cold, tough, competent. As far as she was concerned silence was golden. She would not be seeing him again after this flight. Obviously she was not his sort of person. Maybe she should have come in khaki shorts and knee-length socks, the odd python draped around her neck?

She looked at his hands, long and lean, brown, looking away quickly when he flashed a glance at her as if he could feel her appraisal. It made her heart leap but she wasn't about to scare herself with him. She was scared enough by this swiftly moving toy he called a plane. He had disliked her on sight, and the sooner she got out of his sight, the better.

CHAPTER TWO

IT TOOK all Natalie's courage to look down out of the window but she did it, fascinated in spite of her fears by the changing landscape of Kenya.

They were flying over a lake, where flamingoes rose like a pink cloud only to sink again to their feeding, and she turned her head to watch for as long as possible. She would have liked to ask where they were but of course she was not now on speaking terms with her pilot, a state of affairs that seemed to suit him very well. Kip Forsythe looked vaguely thunderous when she stole a glance at him and she hardly dared look again.

The road ran like a red ribbon below them and she peered down, watching the grassland, the billowing tree-tops and the strange red road.

'It's treacherous in the wet season, sticky mud that makes driving well-nigh impossible. In the dry, it produces clouds of dust like a red fog,' he said tersely. 'The red earth,' he translated when she looked at him in surprise. 'It's not only drunks who see pink elephants; they're down there right now if they cared to step forth and be recognised.'

'Pink?' She looked at him with surprised interest, quite sure he wasn't joking. His tanned face was too severe at the moment to make her imagine that. He was still annoyed with her.

'The watering-holes,' he explained briefly. 'They go into a muddy, wet hole and come out pink.'

'Are there elephants in Madembi?' As he had decided to talk, she thought it very politic to assist a little.

'A few. They don't like change, however, and they eat too much to hang around when buildings are going up almost daily.'

'The result of the prosperity brought by the Kabala Dam,' Natalie mused.

'Partly, and I expect it will get worse. Plenty of animals have suffered.'

'How awful!' She merely voiced a thought but apparently he took it to be some sort of personal insult.

'People have to live too, Miss West,' he informed her coldly. 'Have you ever seen a hungry child?'

'Plenty, Mr Forsythe,' she snapped. 'I don't go around with my eyes permanently closed. We can't alter the things we get on film. We just show it as it is. Once in a while we manage to show up a few injustices too. *That* makes people jump!'

'Oh, Gabriel Basoni is just going to love you, Miss West,' he murmured drily. 'Any skeletons in his cupboard and you're just the lady to find them.'

'I'm here to do a job, at the request of the Madembi government. This is not a prying mission.'

'But anything your flashing green eyes see, the camera will follow,' he assessed astutely. 'Remind me to duck.'

'You're fairly safe,' she pointed out tartly, amazed that she had flashing green eyes. 'I'll never see you. I work hard all the time.'

He gave her a wry look.

'Yes, ma'am! Time will tell.'

Natalie looked away, back out of the window. He infuriated her with his air of supreme self-possession, his aura of power. She felt just as ill as ever but there was one thing at least—she wasn't really scared now;

well, not too much. Temper was useful at times and he could certainly make her temper rise.

'How is your nerve?' he asked after a minute, his voice back to quiet darkness.

'I'm perfectly all right!' She bit out the answer, expecting another taunting interlude.

'Then I'll give you a treat. It may restore your cool composure.'

He put the plane into a dive, not a steep dive but a long shallow one that seemed to be bringing them dangerously close to the ground very quickly. Natalie's hands clenched together tightly, her teeth biting painfully into her lip, a wave of thankfulness flooding over her when he levelled off at tree-top height.

'Good girl,' he said softly. 'No screams, no attempt to wrest the controls from me. For that you get your treat. Look straight ahead.'

They came out of the trees above grassland and Natalie sat up straight, her lips parting in wonder. She had seen giraffes before, but only on film. This time she saw them from close up, settling into their peculiar gait, their oddly undulating run as the herd swept across the grass, disturbed by the small plane.

'Get the glasses.' He motioned to the compartment before her and she took out the binoculars she found there, focusing on the swiftly moving animals, drinking in their colour and movement.

'They've got long eyelashes,' she breathed in awe. 'They're quite beautiful.'

'They are. And quite free, too. I think we've disturbed them enough.' He began to climb and she watched the herd finally slow, mill around and then stop, none the worse apparently for their fright.

'Thank you.' She glanced at him as she packed the binoculars neatly away. 'It was a wonderful sight.'

She received a brilliant, flashing glance from dark eyes.

'Maybe a light aircraft is not so scary as a big jet.'

So, he had been doing his bit towards psychiatric help? It irritated her greatly.

'Perhaps not,' she countered. 'You seem to treat it like a motorbike.' She closed her eyes quickly, wincing as pain jabbed through her head, and he didn't miss her expression.

'You're ill, aren't you?' She took the tone of his voice to be reprimanding, just what she had expected.

'I'm fine. Only tired. I told you that.'

'As you wish,' he murmured scathingly. 'I'll concentrate on getting you to your hotel quickly, Miss West.'

She was sorry then that she hadn't told him just how ill she felt. She was certain he would have helped. It was just that she felt rather vulnerable at the side of him, all that tough, masculine power. In fact she had felt extremely vulnerable from the moment she had opened her eyes at the airport and seen him. He was too big, too golden and bronzed. He had the ability to make her feel inadequate, foolishly feminine and a nuisance he would countenance with amused contempt. There was something almost magnetic about him, hypnotic, as if underneath all that dry derision a powerful dynamo was working, ready to flare into life.

She slept for a while. She had not had the slightest intention of doing so but the steady drone of the aircraft and the feeling of tiredness and weakness combined to make it impossible to keep awake. At least it removed any necessity to speak, and if they were going to have an accident she wouldn't know it.

When she opened her eyes the swift evening was almost upon them. She sat up quickly when she realised she had slid sideways, her head resting against his shoulder. Apart from being embarrassing, it seemed to give him some slight advantage, and he didn't need any of that. She felt wary enough as it was, disturbed by her peculiar response to him; dynamite, waiting for a match.

'Feeling better?' He did not look across when she glanced at him. The red glow of approaching night lit up the small cabin, catching the finely etched planes of his face, darkening his already deep tan, glinting in his fair hair. He looked magnificent really, quite devastating, like no one she had ever seen before.

'Yes, thank you.' The sound of her own voice surprised her; it was thick, raw, and she swallowed uncomfortably, feeling the pain of a sore throat. She would have liked a drink but there didn't seem to be one available.

'There's a Thermos flask behind your seat, if you can reach,' he said quietly. 'It's iced orange. Get it out and have a good drink.'

He was a competent mind reader too. She fished about and managed to reach it, grateful to feel the icy liquid sliding down her throat, putting the flask away when he shook his head at her offer to pour him one.

'I'm looking forward to a stronger drink. We'll be landing in about ten minutes. We entered Madembi quite a while ago. I'll get you settled at once when we land.'

He didn't say it outright, of course, but she could tell he wanted her off his hands with all speed—not that she blamed him. Except for a few minutes they had been on the edge of a fight right from the moment they had met. It made her feel guilty. She didn't really have any right to snap at him. He was obviously not some government servant. He was simply a man who had offered to help out. Belatedly she tried to mend a few fences.

'Thank you for bringing me here.'

'No trouble,' he said suavely. 'I was bringing myself at the same time. I expect you'll be flying out with the rest of your crew when the time comes?'

'Yes. There are four of us. We'll be getting the scheduled flight.'

'And how long will you be here?'

'Not long. The rest of them join me when I'm ready, in about two weeks or maybe less. After that it's speed all the way. Four days will be pushing it. It's quite a costly business. That's why I come to set things up first. It has to go smoothly when the crew get out here. I never told you what I do. It's my job to——'

'I already know what you do,' he interrupted softly. 'You're the hatchet-man for Westwind. The big, strong lady who sets things up.' He was grinning to himself, with a sort of amused malice, and Natalie flushed with annoyance.

It didn't last, though; another wave of dizziness swept over her at the sharp pounding of her head and he said nothing more because they had arrived. She could see the landing lights brilliant against the gathering gloom and once more she gripped her hands tightly together as they began to descend.

When Natalie's feet finally touched the ground, her legs almost folded beneath her and the whole airport lights took on a frightening tendency to spin. It was over in a minute and she managed to hang on grimly but she was thankful when the slight formalities were over and she was being escorted to a dark car parked close to the airport buildings.

It was warm inside, very warm; the stored-up heat from a fierce sun had heated the vehicle in spite of shade from the corrugated roof of the parking bay. He wound down the windows and settled her comfortably before pulling out into the gathering night, the smooth transition from flying a plane to driving no apparent problem. He had every right to his air of self-possession.

She glanced at him secretly. He bothered her and she didn't quite know why. She was quite accustomed to dealing with men, both as boyfriends and as business contacts. Kip Forsythe, though, was like no man she had ever known. It was as if a great precipice yawned between them, every inch of it filled with danger. The bright lights of the airport picked up the clean-cut, masculine face uncannily. In a way he was just a little frightening for no reason she could fathom. He looked as if he would be kind with the right sort of people, but instinct told her she was not in that category. As an enemy he would be pretty ruthless. There was a hard competence about him that showed he could deal with just about anything. He would be gentle with a woman but always slightly disdainful. A man's man, if there was such a thing, although he looked handsome enough to cope in just about any setting.

They were speeding through a sizeable town, the shops still open, and she tried to look around with some interest but gave it up almost at once. She was too weary. As they began to climb steadily the air cooled and she sank back against the seat, feeling safe for the first time since she had left London. Her feet were back on the ground and that was a great comfort.

'If it weren't so late you could see your objective,' the deeply dark voice pointed out. 'The Kabala Dam,' he added when she glanced at him. 'We cross the dam to get to your hotel. The hotel was built on the slope over-looking the dam, a great vantage-point. As it's so late, all you'll see from your hotel window is the lights over the road.'

'It's completely finished, then?' Natalie asked.

'More or less. The official opening is soon but actually it's been partially in action for quite a while. All it needs now is close and careful inspection and Africans trained to take care of it.'

The car jolted over a patch of rough ground and Natalie clutched her head, unable to help herself, pain shooting through her like small knives.

He glanced at her sharply. 'Have you anything with you for that headache?'

'No.' Actually, she hadn't admitted to a headache, but not a lot escaped him.

'Then we'll make a small detour. I live close by and I can't guarantee that the hotel will have anything, splendid modern structure notwithstanding.'

She almost told him she was all right but he didn't look as if he would take kindly to untruths at this stage and she certainly needed something, so she kept quiet and soon they were turning into the drive of a house set back off the road.

Lights were on outside, lighting up the drive and grounds, and she could see that it was quite a big house, one-storeyed in the old colonial manner, white, red-roofed and surrounded by verandas. It stood in what appeared to be a sizeable garden and they stopped at a flight of long steps that fronted the house.

'Come inside. I'll get you a couple of tablets. You can take them now.'

He was not expecting any disobedience and didn't look as if he ever would expect it. He came round to help her out, taking her arm and leading the way to the front door where a plump, dark-faced man suddenly appeared like a beaming genie.

'Get some water, Josh, and then make the lady a tray of tea.'

Natalie turned to protest. She had the greatest desire to jerk her arm away from the cool, firm grasp but common sense told her to go carefully. He bothered her. It was ridiculous but a definite fact nevertheless. She moved out of his reach surreptitiously, swinging round.

'Really, there's no need. If I could just have the water...'

She never heard the reply because everything began to swim dizzily again and as he turned to speak to her she fainted at his feet, sliding to the hard, polished floor before he could catch her, the crack her head received chasing any remaining reality completely away.

Natalie was lying on a long settee when she opened her eyes. The soft lights from lamps hurt her, her head ached unbelievably and she struggled to sit up.

'Stay right where you are.' The swift command brought her completely back to the present and she turned her head to see Kip Forsythe bending over her, his face somewhat grim.

'What happened?' She screwed up her eyes to see him and as if he understood the pain he crouched down beside her.

'For somebody who's perfectly all right, you have a good line in fainting. I'm afraid you took me by surprise. I wasn't quite fast enough and you banged your head considerably. That's not going to help.'

'I've never fainted before.' Natalie looked at him wonderingly. She felt too ill to worry about her own vulnerability now, sick and aching, this far place not home, no help to hand. If he hadn't been so uncompromisingly masculine she would have had a little weep.

'There's always a first time.' He stood up and looked down at her, dark eyes slipping over her face, seeing far too much. 'Close your eyes for a minute and the doctor will be here when you open them.'

'I don't think I need a doctor...'

'Stick to your own profession and leave him to his. I would guess that if you move at all you'll faint again so there's not a lot we can do about it. We'll wait and see what happens, shall we?'

A suave question that sounded like an order. She was beginning to understand why he looked so commanding. He was used to being obeyed. Right now she was almost grateful but later she would resent it, she knew that for sure.

'I've been a lot of trouble,' she began apologetically.

'I expect nothing else from a beautiful woman. Stop worrying.' His voice held a mixture of amusement and impatience. 'You look extremely vulnerable, lying there. Nothing could touch the male heart-strings more. If you could manage to control that sharp tongue, I'd be fascinated.'

There was just something in his tone that stung, in spite of his apparent kindness. Maybe he just didn't like women? *She* was stuck with him anyway—a tough, golden stranger, and she felt so awfully ill. A bit of self-pity flared up and her green eyes filled with tears, a fact he didn't miss.

'It's all right.' He looked down at her with amused compassion. 'I've got a baby sister of my own, not much older than you. I'll treat you accordingly.'

The dark glance seemed to glitter right over her and she felt some shiver of reaction, almost primeval. It was humiliating to have to lie there with no strength to take evasive action. He looked dangerously male, an ironic quirk to those carved lips, and a flush ran over her skin even though she felt so ill.

'I won't need looking after,' she managed shakily, but all she got was a peculiar stare that went right through her.

'You'll always need looking after. Whoever gets the pleasure had better not mistake your tough attitude. I don't think there's a lot to back it up, Miss West.'

The doctor was old, his wrinkled skin the colour of walnut, the sort of Englishman who had spent his life in Africa and would never leave.

'Virus,' he said with every appearance of satisfaction. 'Two or three days and it will burn itself out.' He did not speak to Natalie. His remarks were addressed to Kip Forsythe as if Natalie were an inanimate object; he was another 'man's man' apparently. 'Get her to bed and keep her there. Plenty to drink, no upsets and give her these.' He handed over some tablets and made for the door, stopping as an afterthought came to him. 'Oh, yes, just keep a careful eye on her this evening. That bang on the head may be a trouble. There's a very nice lump there so I don't expect she'll suffer more than a bad head but watch her. Call me if you need me.'

He just walked out and Natalie watched with dazed eyes, biting her lip when she saw Kip Forsythe come back into the room and look at her determinedly.

'Two or three days? I've got work to do!'

'Not at the moment. As things stand you'll be lucky to get anything done for a week. It's fortunate we flew in. A long drive here would have just about finished you off and you would have been stuck across country in a hotel with no help at all.'

'I'm stuck now,' she protested feebly, but all she got was a wry look.

'No, you're not. Help is right here, just about to follow the doctor's orders and put you to bed.'

He lifted her like a child, her slender height nothing to him at all as he walked determinedly from the room.

'I can't stay here—with *you*!' Her shocked whisper amused him, the hard planes of his face softening into laughter as he glanced down at her.

'I have more than one bed, I assure you. Even if I hadn't I would certainly give it up for you. I'm a gentleman of the old school. Ladies in distress and sick children a speciality—dragons killed to order.'

'But people will...' Her anxious words died away at his wry expression, faint colour flooding into her face as wicked laughter flashed in his dark eyes.

'The house is pretty isolated,' he told her in a conspiratorial murmur. 'I'll keep you tucked up here and nobody will even know I've got you.'

Natalie was too weak to struggle and in any case she knew he was simply taunting her. She had never felt so helpless before and tears glazed her green eyes again. It was hateful of him to be like this when she was in no condition to retaliate. She had known what he would be like the moment she had seen him at the airport.

'You're not very nice.' Her voice trembled and he looked down at her quickly, his amusement dying at once.

'I'm nice when the need arises.' His eyes held hers as he shouldered his way into a lamplit room. 'Don't go tearful on me, Natalie. You're a brisk television lady, remember? We'll bear that in mind and all will be well.'

'I feel awful!' There was a catch in her voice and she despised the self-pity but it came out all the same.

'I know.' His arms just tightened slightly, an odd feeling of warmth flowing into her as if he was giving her some of his superb strength. He lowered her to a soft bed. 'We'll get you into bed and then give you a couple of the tablets. A good sleep will help quite a lot.'

'How do you know my name?' Irrelevant thoughts seemed to be floating to the top of her mind. She felt dizzy, ridiculously helpless.

'If you remember, you introduced yourself. In any case, I had your name when I came to collect you. No description, though.' He frowned slightly. 'That seemed to be a State secret.' She could see that the thought annoyed him and she gasped and tried to move away as he began to 'get her into bed', his strong lean hands on her ankles as he slipped off her sandals.

'I can manage!'

Her anxious assertion brought dark eyes back to hers as he leaned over and looked at her with some exasperation.

'Right! Go ahead!' He stood back and she looked up at him from her almost collapsed position on the bed.

'Well, you'll have to go out,' she managed breathlessly.

'Well, I will,' he countered. 'Just try to call out before you hit the floor again. I'm not quite sure how many bangs a head like yours can take.'

He strode off to the door and she sat up, her head reeling, waves of nausea washing over her. Her dress fastened at the back and she ached so much that trying to reach the zip was like an Olympic effort. She lay back and closed her eyes. She would sleep like this. It didn't much matter.

'Uncrushable or not, that dress comes off.' The determined voice made her wince and she saw him standing looking down at her, the lights catching the brilliant shine of fair hair. He must have been able to move like a panther because she had never heard him come back.

'I can't do it.'

'I didn't expect you could.' He sounded very exasperated and sat beside her, lifting her up to lean back against him, his hand on her zip.

'You—you can't...' Her protest annoyed him and the zip plunged down with a speed that showed his exasperation had turned to displeasure.

'It's either me or Josh,' he rasped. 'We're landed with you and we'll deal with you. I would imagine that a girl like you has been undressed before. Set your mind at rest. I don't attack the sick and weak.'

'I—I didn't think you did. It's just that... Ooh!'

Tears spilled down her cheeks, pain, weakness and this ridiculous situation getting the better of her. If she had been feeling all right she would have hit him at that remark about being undressed. If he couldn't see that she was fastidious then he was stupid. She tried to wipe the tears from her cheeks, giving herself away, and his hold on her gentled.

'Hey! No tears. You're perfectly safe.'

'I—I know that. It's because...'

'Because you feel absolutely rotten and you're embarrassed. I'll be the soul of discretion. Close your eyes and pretend I'm not there.'

Well, she *did* try it but the touch of his hands on her skin gave her a small electric shock. He slid the dress to her waist and then unclipped her bra, resting her against him as he turned and pulled her suitcase from the end of the bed.

'Is this locked?' he asked gruffly, and Natalie shook her head slightly, her long, black hair parting and falling forward. She knew her nightie was on top and in a second he had eased her away, sliding the cool silk over her head and letting it fall around her. He stood her up, resting her against him, lifting her clear of the dress that fell to the floor.

His fingers on the fastening of her waist slip made her shiver; they lightly touched her stomach, cool and firm, and then he was gently pulling her arms into the nightie and lifting her back to bed.

'There. Very discreet, The best nursing care. It's all over.' He looked down at her steadily, his lips slightly curving in a smile. 'After that, the rest should be easy.'

It had exhausted her and she made no fuss when he handed her two tablets and a drink.

'What are they?' She looked at him with pain-filled eyes, too weak to be embarrassed, anyway, it was done now.

He glanced at the bottle. 'Painkillers. Try to sleep now.'

He turned to go but she still felt very guilty about the way she had behaved, almost as if she had no control over herself. It was not the image she liked to project. In some weird way it seemed to be his fault but her head, aching though it was, informed her that she was entirely to blame. She just hadn't acted normally with him. It was as if she had been instinctively led to fight him on sight.

'Mr Forsythe. I'm sorry.'

'Kip.' He turned his fair head and looked down at her. 'I can't have my guest being so formal. If we get visitors it will make everything look so much more suspicious.'

There was a taunting look about him but she was very wary because underneath she felt sure he was angry, very angry, and as she was the only one here it had to be with her.

Later, she was sure. When he came back she kept her eyes closed although the pain in her head had not in any way eased. She knew he was standing looking down at her but she must have fooled him because he switched off all but one lamp and went out, leaving the door only a little ajar. She began to drift into sleep but the sound of his voice woke her after a few minutes. It was low but she could hear him quite clearly, hear the angry undertone even though there was still that mocking quality to it.

'Oh, yes, Mr Minister, sir. I have your television lady. She's right here, safe but not altogether sound.'

'Why, it's really good of you to thank me,' he drawled sarcastically after listening for a second. 'There are more glad tidings, though. Your tough, businesslike advance guard is ill. No, she's *not* in hospital! She's not bad enough for hospital and not good enough for a hotel so guess where she is? Right first time! Oh, no, it's no trouble at all, think nothing of it.' He gave a sort of low growl. 'Damn you, Gabe! You're a sneaky devil! I did you a favour after much persuasion. I went to pick up a middle-aged woman in battle-dress with a few cameras slung over her shoulder; *that* was your offhand description. What I've got is an exotic black and gold butterfly. If you think I'm riding shotgun on her while she's here—think again. I've got enough on my plate as it is and I can tell you this, she'll never survive. She's stepped right out of a dream. One blast of reality and she'll be blown away.'

Natalie felt the tablets working, making her drift far away, her urge to get up and join in the conversation fading as fast as her ability to keep listening. An exotic black and gold butterfly! Temper made her more sick than ever. Just let him wait! She would put that taunting devil right in his place—just as soon as she was better...

In the night, pain woke her. She was already moaning as she opened her eyes and she bit her lips tightly together to stop the sound as Kip got up quickly from an easy chair by the bed. It hadn't been there before. He must have brought it in as she slept.

He was beside her at once, handing her a drink and more tablets.

'Here we go.' He glanced at his watch. 'It's just about time.' He eased his arm under her, lifting her so that she could drink, lying her back down when the tablets were safely swallowed.

For a moment she just looked at him, slightly puzzled, feeling more than a little woozy. He looked back at her steadily, his eyes skimming over her face.

'How do you feel?'

'Dreadful, though I hate to admit it.'

He smiled, his hand coming to brush the black hair from her face with a gentleness that surprised her, taking her nuisance value into consideration.

'You'll feel better tomorrow, no doubt, although I'm not a very experienced nurse.' He moved, sitting back in the chair, resting his head back and closing his eyes. 'Off to sleep, Natalie.'

'What are you doing here?' She kept her eyes on him, green and weary but very puzzled.

'Watching your head. You heard the doctor.' He did not open his eyes and the mocking voice was the same as ever, low, dark and taunting. She remembered the telephone call then, the crack about her appearance.

'There's no need for you to stay.' Her voice was meant to be sharp, but under the circumstances it came out a bit trembly. He opened dark eyes and looked straight at her.

'But I *want* to watch your head, Natalie. It's so beautiful. You can sleep in the sure knowledge that I won't take my eyes off it.' He closed his eyes at once and she turned over, every movement painful. When she was better she would pay him back in full. She would also offer to pay for her keep here. That would annoy him! The thought gave her a lot of consolation.

As it turned out, she was quite ill for two days, only vaguely aware of what went on around her. The doctor came several times and she could tell by the tone of Kip's voice that he had insisted. The doctor didn't seem at all interested whether she lived or died. Naturally Kip cared a great deal. As it was she presented a problem. If anything further happened to her his fury would know no bounds. She could just see the headlines—'Television woman dies in house of white...' What? She had no idea what he did, why he was out here in Madembi. It irritated her inquisitive mind. She was slipping up. Normally she would have had his life story out of him within the first half-hour. It wasn't just the virus and she knew it. Since meeting him she had been trying to keep him out of her mind with an almost desperate determination.

CHAPTER THREE

A NEW black face joined the establishment, a round female face that looked on Natalie with pity, capable hands that changed her sheets and nightie. Apart from a few minutes each afternoon and evening she saw nothing of Kip and she guessed that whatever he did for a living he was off out and doing it.

On the third day, Natalie got up. She felt very weak and decidedly groggy but she got up all the same, dismissing the outraged cluckings of Josh and the newly acquired Mina who turned out to be Josh's wife. She made it to the cool veranda at the front of the house and sat in her thin robe on the rattan chair, drinking in the sight of a quite beautiful garden.

It stretched to the road as she had realised the night she had arrived, the tall hedge around it guarding the whole property from prying eyes. There were thick bushes of bougainvillaea, the bright red and purple blossoms spilling to the ground. Tall trees were dotted around, some with fruit that she assumed were mangoes, and the garden itself was alive with orange lilies and white daisies.

She sat with the tray of tea that Josh brought to her and listened to the song of the birds. Everything was lush, heavy with moist air, but it was beautiful and peaceful. Further down the lawn, the gardener was cutting the grass, his strong arm swinging rhythmically as he wielded a quite ferocious-looking scythe.

Peace was shattered as a Land Rover, well covered with dust, pulled into the drive and roared up to the front of the house. There was something angry about the sound of it and she almost cringed as Kip got out, rounding the bonnet in long swinging strides, his frown quite alarming.

'What the devil are you doing up?' He glared down at her and Natalie gathered her courage to look back at him fearlessly. He looked quite furious, not the softly taunting man she had become used to. He was in khaki shirt and trousers, the shirt sleeves rolled up over brown forearms, the crisp, tough khaki making him look quite alien to her as if he was a stranger all over again. His hair was incredibly fair against the khaki and she couldn't seem to take her eyes off him.

'I felt better. I can't go on hanging around in bed.'

'It's only been two days, for heaven's sake!' he snapped, glaring at her more. He raised his voice and bellowed for Josh, who came at a run. 'Get me a cold beer, Josh. Lunch in fifteen minutes,' he ordered. He dropped down to a seat facing Natalie.

'You are to get completely better,' he grated. 'That's not a suggestion. It's an order.'

'From the minister of culture?' she asked quietly. It made him look surprised.

'Why the hell should it be?' he bit out. 'Gabriel Basoni is a friend of mine, not my boss.'

'I see. You help him to collect butterflies. I understand.' For a second he just looked right at her, seeing the growing irritation in the jewelled green eyes, and then he smiled tauntingly.

'Of course, you listen in to other people's telephone calls. Naturally you trained for that. I expect it's part of your job.'

'It's no such thing!' Natalie blazed at him. She had tried the taunting herself and failed. Kip was the expert and now he only looked more taunting than ever.

'A personal preference; well, I never! You're so sweet and delicate-looking that I would never have believed it!'

She glared into the mocking darkness of his eyes, her face beginning to turn from a pale olive to a fiery red.

'I'll leave today, Mr Forsythe,' she informed him stiffly. 'You've been very kind to me in spite of your annoyance and I'm grateful. I can go to my hotel now, though, and I'll leave after lunch.'

He stood and towered over her, holding her embarrassed gaze with great ease.

'Oh, no, you won't, butterfly,' he assured her. 'You'll leave when I say so. I'm not having all my good work ruined because you've got more spirit than sense. I'd only have to bring you back here again and put you to bed. I have other things to do.'

He left her open-mouthed. He couldn't order her about! Josh came in to announce lunch and Kip nodded to him, never taking his eyes off Natalie.

'You can sit at the table and eat lunch with me if you're very good later,' he offered sardonically, as if she was a child who needed coaxing.

She was just going to tell him what he could do when he bent and swept her up into his arms, walking along the veranda and into the house.

'Put me down!' she muttered, filled with shame as both Josh and Mina stood grinning widely.

'But why? I really enjoy this. It's worth the trip home at lunchtime just to hold you. It could make a good hobby.' He sat her at the table and sank to the opposite chair, smiling tauntingly into her outraged eyes. 'Slacken off, Natalie,' he said quietly. 'You know I'm teasing. You're not in any way ready to face work, or a hotel. Give it a few more days.'

She looked away, feeling shaky, strangely stirred by his hold over her.

'Taunting and teasing are two different things. You taunt!'

'I'll try not to. I wouldn't want to hurt a little black kitten.'

'Perhaps you'd better make up your mind just what sort of creature I am,' Natalie snapped, back to normal at the slightly patronising tone.

He looked at her steadily. 'A fascinating creature,' he answered, getting on with his soup and ignoring her completely from then on, his mind obviously on other things.

After that, Natalie was up every day, although sometimes she was forced to take an afternoon nap. She soon pushed off the virus but she knew she was not well enough to start work yet. At Kip's insistence, she rang her father, getting him to ring back and chat. It was not much of a chat. Of course he was worried but as soon as she told him she was almost better he began to remind her about the opening date of the Kabala Dam, the tight schedule, told her all over again what she must do and thoroughly irritated her until she snapped at him.

When she walked back into the lamplit lounge Kip was reading but his lips were quirking. Of course he had heard—he could hardly have failed to. She had raised her voice several times before the final outburst.

'Don't accuse me of eavesdropping,' he warned when she looked at him with exasperation.

'I wasn't about to. I realise you couldn't miss that. When my father gets under way he has to be stopped smartly.'

'And you stopped him fine.' He threw down his book. 'Tell me what you do.'

'I do all the research.' Natalie sat opposite, not so uneasy when she could talk about her job. 'I did that in television before I joined Westwind Productions. My father wouldn't have me until I was trained and by that time I wasn't too keen to leave my own job. He persuaded me, though, and I have to admit I enjoy it.'

'So you make notes?' He was stretched out on the long rattan settee, resting back against the cushions. 'What else?'

'We plan everything in the studio but once out on the job I change things as and when necessary and make out a final working plan. I make notes for the commentary and set up the camera shots. Of course, Ray sometimes changes those, but by and large I know how his mind works and manage to satisfy his whims.'

'Ray?' He looked at her steadily and she lifted slender shoulders in a delicate shrug.

'The cameraman. He's good.'

'What do the others do?'

'Producer and sound among other things. Being a small company, we double up on jobs.' Her mind slid to Paula, who also doubled as Neil's assistant.

'All men?' He was watching so intently that she had to look away. Now that she was better the thought of Neil was eating into her again and she wondered if it showed. She would have to face him soon.

'One woman, besides me.'

He nodded, still watching her, and she had to stand up, agitation suddenly making her restless. It was ironic that she would be the one to tell them to come out here. It would have been better if she had left the company altogether but that would have been more than obvious to her father and to Neil. This break away from him hadn't done anything to help. She was both dying to see him and dreading it. It would have been better if she could have hated Paula but who could hate a bubbly-haired child? She couldn't help thinking of Paula like that and she often thought that that was what had attracted Neil to her.

'Can I walk to the gate? Is it safe?' Suddenly she wanted to run, hide, refuse to face anything else.

'Safe enough, just the odd bat. I'll come with you.' He stood slowly, following when she moved out on to the veranda and down the steps. It was lovely and cool, the heavy moisture not seeming to be there any more. The stars were brilliant against a deep velvet sky, the Southern Cross hanging like jewels in the dark.

'It's beautiful,' Natalie breathed. 'How long have you lived here?'

'On and off, five years. More on than off.'

She wanted him to talk about himself but he never did. She too had kept her life very much a secret. Even so he knew more about her than she did about him. She knew nothing at all. He didn't volunteer any information now and she didn't ask. He wasn't very comfortable to be with and it was not only the sure knowledge that she irritated him. She was always alert with him. She couldn't chatter to him. She was much too shy, in spite of her businesslike appearance, and he was too enigmatic, too rawly masculine.

Sometimes he was mockingly gentle but not very often. More often than not he was totally unreachable, a man alone, self-confident and cool. His mockery covered irritation as far as she was concerned, but he was much too civilised to show it.

'Do you always live by yourself?' she asked rather foolishly, blurting out the thought when it surfaced, following the idea that had been in her mind for a couple of days. There must be a woman somewhere in the life of a man like this. He was too potently male to be denied.

'Not always,' he murmured. 'Right now I live with you.'

Natalie blushed, thankful it was dark.

'Very funny! It was a silly question, anyway. You're too tough to fall in love.' She felt horrified when she heard her own words. Whatever had got into her? In the first place it was impertinent and in the second place she was just asking for trouble.

'Love? What's that?' He took her arm and swung her to face him as they reached the wide gates.

'I—I'm sorry. It was very rude. I don't know why I said it.'

'Oh? I do. You're inquisitive, a further part of your training. Maybe I should tell you in case you want to make some of those notes. I can't count the number of times I've been in love. Sometimes it lasted a night, sometimes a whole two days.'

'A convenient excuse for sex, you mean?' Natalie retaliated, swinging away. She had asked for this, blurting out such odd thoughts. She should have known better with Kip Forsythe.

'Who needs an excuse?' He caught her arm again, swinging her back to face him, his hands coming lightly to her shoulders. 'Now you, you're doing very well, butterfly. I've been in love with you for all of five days.'

He was laughing down at her and it not only infuriated her, it scared her. His hands were absently moulding her delicate shoulders, his lean brown fingers tracing the bones, and she felt a wave of unaccustomed emotion, like heat, uncomfortable and unacceptable. She started to tremble, a panic-stricken feeling bubbling up very close to the surface.

'You're trembling, Natalie.' His hands still moulded her slender shoulders, carefully, as if he thought she might break. 'What are you afraid of? You think I'd be brutal?'

'I'm going back inside.' She couldn't control her voice and it trembled too.

'Because you're afraid? It's really only fear of the unknown.'

He pulled her completely into his arms, folding her against him, looking down at her, the lights from the house catching his fair hair, and she stiffened immediately, much too aware of the hard body close to hers. He hadn't behaved like this before and suddenly he was dangerous, as if a restraint had been lifted. Maybe because she had been ill he had never...

'I won't have an affair with you!' She spoke wildly, shaking too much to pull away, terribly aware of being in a foreign land, of being close to a hard handsome stranger.

'Why, Natalie,' he mocked. 'Wait until you're asked.' His hand cupped her head, threading through her long black hair. 'Be still. I've never held such a delicate girl.'

'*Please*, Kip!' It was the first time she had ever actually used his name and the sound of it shocked her as if she was inviting some great intimacy.

Before she could put up any sort of fight his glittering head bent and his lips caught hers, taking her by surprise. She didn't even have time to think. It was nothing she had expected, so sweet, so possessive that she was powerless to move, a very forbidden delight swelling up inside. He trailed his lips across hers, his tongue stroking the corner of her mouth, holding her in a sort of spell for a second. Vaguely her mind compared it with Neil's kisses and fright hit her badly. Neil had been careful, gentle, asking nothing. The lips over her own were sensuous, probing and questioning, arousing a riotous sexuality inside her for all their care. He ran his hand down her spine and she almost collapsed against him before self-preservation surfaced.

She pulled clear and just ran, her heart pounding like a drum. She fled across the grass, giving a little cry of panic as he caught her and swept her off her feet into his arms.

'Put me down!' Her small fists pummelled him but he walked calmly to the path, letting her feet touch the ground at once.

'Don't panic. Honestly, I'm busy. For any affair, you'll just have to wait.' He grasped her head, taking her long hair and winding it around his hand, pulling her face up to his, and she was terrified he would kiss her again. The thought of that, the fear and the shamefully exciting hope were silenced as he suddenly smiled sardonically. 'Don't go on the grass at night in sandals,' he ordered quietly, letting her go. 'There are snakes.'

She almost jumped back into his arms but he didn't laugh, he meant it, and she turned her head to look with great suspicion at the lawn, trembling as he led her towards the house.

'Stop shivering. Nothing bit you, not even me.' His voice was dark with mocking amusement and she flushed with shame.

'I'll go to the hotel tomorrow,' she muttered, her head down to escape those dark eyes.

'Agreed.' His voice was both matter-of-fact and commanding. 'Not that you're not welcome here, but it's safer all round if you move now you're well. I might just get attached to you.'

Not in a million years! His opinion of women was obvious without any chauvinistic comments. In fact he was above making comments like that, the sort of things she'd heard all her adult life. His amused eyes and his taunting looks said more than any snide remarks.

She went to her room without facing him again, his final words ringing in her mind.

'I'll drive you up to the hotel after lunch tomorrow.'

Well, it couldn't come soon enough. Men like that worried her. Neil was so very different: quiet, thoughtful, loving. Tears came flooding into her eyes. What was she thinking? Neil didn't belong to her any more; he never had done. Her father had said they would be 'mooning about'. It seemed to her that she would be the one doing that if she didn't pull herself together.

Her treacherous mind slid back to Kip, defying her determination to forget all about him. She could feel his hands on her, his mouth over hers. He almost seemed to be there still and her tongue ran over her lips, searching sensuously for the taste of him, a low cry of shock coming from her throat when she realised just what she was doing. She seemed to have gone quite mad out here. He had been laughing at her in his hateful way, laughing at her all the time.

The next morning she rang up about hiring a car. She was going to need one and if she could get one now she could drive herself up to the hotel. Of course there wasn't one until the evening but they promised to deliver it to the hotel. It had to satisfy her. She packed and then had nothing at all to do. She put on white jeans and a bright red shirt and went to wander around the garden, keeping a wary look-out for snakes and any other nasties.

She was interested because she did a fair amount of gardening at home. Some of the plants were familiar, though about twice as big as the ones in England's cold climate. She snapped off dead heads almost absent-mindedly, nodding pleasantly to the African gardener who was working further away and giving her odd looks.

If she didn't get away from here soon she would be getting some very odd looks indeed. She had been swept up into the house of a stranger and cared for like a child; even undressed, she remembered in embarrassment. He hadn't treated her like a child last night. It still clung to her.

She snapped off some dead twigs from one of the bushes and jumped with shock as the gardener started to shout at her and run towards her like a maniac. She wondered what was wrong with him until she saw the black ants that covered her arms. They were pouring out from the broken twigs with unbelievable speed and she was too stunned to drop the source of danger.

She hadn't heard the Land Rover come in. The shouting had held her in a sort of startled suspense because Josh had joined in too, running from the house, and now Kip came towards her, grabbing her, knocking the dead twigs from her arms and shouting orders to Mina.

'Fill the bathroom basin!'

He almost hurled her towards the house and it dawned on her why. She was being bitten unmercifully, the ants resisting Josh's attempts to brush them off. It was like white-hot needles and as they reached the bathroom Kip plunged her arms into the basin of cold water that Mina had already prepared.

He was swearing very fluently under his breath as he dealt with them but she was not at all better. They were up her sleeves, biting her shoulders, in her long hair, and Kip took in the situation swiftly.

'Under the shower!' He turned it on and pushed her under the sharp jets, clothes and all. 'Let that water get all over. They don't like water. I'll get your wrap.'

He strode out and Natalie began to peel off her clothes, shuddering with distaste. She stood with the water streaming down her, her clothes on the floor of the shower, the water flooding through her long hair. The horrid little things! Their speed had scared her more than anything else. How could she have been so stupid, treating an African garden like a cool, suburban patch in England? The bites were burning like small fires.

She stepped out, reaching for a towel, freezing as Kip's voice came close.

'Natalie, you've packed your robe. I've got you one of mine. You can get those clothes off now...' He was in the doorway before he realised she had already pulled off her clothes, his eyes sweeping over her with dark disbelief. 'I'm sorry. I thought...'

Natalie just stared at him, too stunned to move, waiting for a blast of annoyance to hit her, holding the towel like a very inadequate shield. She hadn't had the shield there as he had walked in and she could still feel the dark gaze that had roamed over her, lingering on her darkened nipples, down her slender legs. All she could think of was that she had annoyed and embarrassed Kip as well as herself.

He wasn't annoyed. He wasn't even embarrassed. He just turned off the shower and handed her the robe, his eyes never moving from hers.

'Don't panic,' he said huskily. 'I'm not going to touch you. Get into the robe.' His dark eyes swept from the rise of her breasts to the long, wet hair that flowed down her back. 'Put a towel round your hair and come straight out. I'll put some lotion on the bites and you can have some hot tea. You've had a shock—two shocks,' he added under his breath as he left.

He didn't know how much of a shock! Nobody had ever seen her like that before. She was filled with shame, trying to remember exactly how she had looked as he had walked in so innocently, his only thought to see to her comfort. Another day here and she would probably die of shame.

Kip didn't allow her to. He gave her tea, a brandy and a short, sharp lecture on the difference between England and Africa while he smoothed cooling lotion on to her arms. He even allowed Josh to hang around and listen, his face stern with agreement although he had never been to England in his life.

By the time Kip had finished she felt all of eight years old and therefore perfectly safe standing about wet and naked in a shower with the door open. She also felt furious, doubly so because she had to take everything he flung at her and nod obediently since it was all true. When he told her he would now drive her to the hotel she couldn't get out of the house fast enough.

She informed him somewhat pithily that by evening she would have a car of her own. He was not unduly impressed when she told him how she had ordered it. No doubt he thought she should have gone to town and inspected every hire car, spanner in hand? She was beginning to wonder about the women he knew. They must be simpering fools. No wonder he felt the need to dominate.

*   *   *

As Kip drove her to the Kabala Hotel after lunch, Natalie started to realise just how isolated she had been for the past few days. With very little effort, her world had become the house, the garden and Kip.

Now, as they drove along the road to the hotel she saw all the signs of the beginning of prosperity that her father had surmised would follow the building of the giant Kabala Dam. There were more cars than she had anticipated, more houses, neat bungalows, still in the colonial style but not so grand as Kip's house, which was old. Shops stretched well out of the main town and she could see laughing groups of black schoolchildren returning to school for the afternoon, their bright blue uniforms colourful. Prosperity had already begun, and all because engineers had built a dam.

That was another thing she would have to do. Mallory-Carter, the great Canadian firm who had built the Kabala Dam, had a representative out here. The Minister, Gabriel Basoni, had told her father he would put her in touch with this man, but so far she had heard nothing of him. It would be good to get him on film; besides, she needed his expertise.

She was silent. Not only were the sights new and interesting but she was still feeling uneasy about Kip. The thought of the incident in the bathroom refused to leave her mind. As far as he was concerned it had never happened but she was not in any doubt that it had. For one thing, her skin still had a tendency to tingle when she thought of it. Although he had been very civilised, his dark eyes had burned a trail over her, devouring her as she had stood there so shockingly vulnerable. Suddenly the handsome, taunting face had been filled with masculine sensuality, light flaring behind the darkness of his eyes.

Worse still was the lingering feeling that had flashed through her when he had calmed her and assured her he was not about to touch her. It had been an almost painful disappointment. Physically she was attracted to Kip Forsythe and she knew it quite well. It was a dangerous attraction that had nothing to do with anything but chemistry. She had never felt it before in her life and it left her extremely wary. It was an uncomfortable feeling, not at all how she felt about Neil.

'Around the next bend you'll see your target,' Kip said quietly when she sat beside him and said nothing at all. 'Your first sight of the dam.'

Nearly immediately they rounded the bend and she gasped with an almost frightened awe. The enormous was always intimidating and she had expected nothing at all like this.

Madembi was a country of high, jungle-clad hills that watched over the plains, the flat bushland that ran to the border and beyond. It had many rivers, wide and swift-flowing, bringing floods and devastation in the rains, and the greatest of these rivers had been harnessed to serve the whole country. The Kabala River had wrought havoc in its history but it had been diverted to allow for the building of this giant dam. Now it had been returned to its own path, shackled, controlled and disciplined by an enormous man-made construction, the giant Kabala Dam.

Natalie was stunned as she saw it, her green eyes wide with awe. It stood white and mighty against the back-cloth of green, its sheer size overwhelming as it spanned the river, curving into each bank like a great bow. The road ran along the top and she could see cars passing across, so many toys at the side of the sheer size of the dam. Even from this distance there was the sound of falling water as the great river was forced to comply with man's decisions. Sunlight caught the cascades that fell to the lower level, rainbows glittering in the light.

She could see this on film at once and she turned to Kip, grasping his arm, never taking her eyes from the dam.

'Please stop!' It was a stunned whisper and he glanced at her curiously, seeing the fervent look on her face. He pulled to the side of the road and she was out of the car at once, her camera snatched from the bag that contained her equipment. This was a shot to start the whole documentary. The sight, the sound, the magnificent, terrifying splendour of it.

Utterly oblivious to anything else, Natalie took the shots she wanted, climbing a nearby wall to angle the camera better as Kip watched with narrowed, dark eyes, seeing her as he had not seen her before. Even her body language was different. She was a professional, ignoring the fascinated schoolchildren who risked being late to watch her. Her hands pushed her hair back impatiently, her face flushed with excitement when she finally came back to the Land Rover and climbed inside.

'Thank you.' Her voice was breathless with enthusiasm and he smiled slowly, his eyes skimming her vibrant figure, her glowing face.

'So you really know what you're doing,' he murmured, meeting her surprised gaze as she looked across at him.

'Of course I do. I go all over the world. I never know where I'll be next.'

'A bit tricky when you marry.'

Her face closed as if it were a flower hiding from the light. 'I doubt if that problem is going to arise.' There was a stiff sound to her voice that had his eyes narrowing again.

'How old are you, Natalie?'

'Twenty-four.' On the edge of gloom she answered without thought. It would not have been tricky with Neil. They were both in the same business. They had even discussed it.

'You're merely a babe,' he commented wryly. 'There's plenty of time to fall in love again.'

'What do you mean—again? I've never been in love. You're the one with expertise in that direction!' She was alert at once, defensive, cool and his lips twisted ironically.

'Merely an excuse for sex, or so you told me. *You*, now, have been hit very badly. What went wrong?'

'With your imagination, you should be writing books,' Natalie assured him drily, being careful not to meet the dark eyes. 'I'm dedicated to my job. It's the only excitement I need.'

'I think we've disproved that already, but, in case you're still in doubt, we'll keep in touch.'

She didn't trust herself to speak and he turned to the dam, saying nothing, allowing her to drink in the sight of it. The great wide road that crossed over the top was part of the dam itself, curving to reach the opposite bank, and halfway over Kip stopped the Land Rover, getting out and coming to open her door.

'Make the most of it. Take some more shots,' he suggested.

Natalie got out but she was very uneasy and looked it. 'I don't want to get off on the wrong foot here. I'm going to need a lot of co-operation.'

'I thought I *was* co-operating.' He looked down at her with some amusement and she looked quickly away from the dark, smiling eyes.

'I wasn't meaning you. You must know there's a notice at the beginning of this road that says "No stopping over the dam".'

'Oh, that.' He shrugged dismissively, walking to the edge and signalling her to follow. 'That's not for me. I stop when I want and where I want.'

'Because you're a friend of the minister?' Natalie asked, a little more easy in her mind.

He grinned, white teeth gleaming against a tanned face, fair hair caught by the strong sunlight.

'No, ma'am. I do as I like because I'm in charge of this tame monster. I even helped to build the thing.'

'You!' She just stared at him and he leaned back against the protective rail, the awesome mass of water a backdrop to his amused elegance.

'Now, why do you *do* that?' Dark eyes laughed at her, amused at her open-mouthed astonishment. 'It's just what you said when I offered to fly you out here. You seem to imagine I'm incompetent.'

Oh, no, she didn't! Whatever he did she had been sure it was both competent and important. It was just that this had never occurred to her. He hadn't told her either, even though he had known she was out here because of the dam—*his* dam!

CHAPTER FOUR

'YOU might have told me!' Natalie gave Kip a small, green-eyed glare that amused him even more.

'I thought I'd keep something in reserve in case you lost interest in me,' he volunteered, and that got a very quick retort, even though her face flushed swiftly.

'Believe me, I'm *not* interested in you. I appreciate your kindness and now, of course, I'll have to see something of you to get details of the dam. But don't go thinking that... Anyway,' she finished in lame embarrassment as he simply watched her mockingly, 'the minister told my father he would get me in touch with the person in charge.'

'Didn't he just, though?' Kip murmured sardonically. 'Gabriel Basoni has an overdeveloped sense of humour.'

'I—I'm sorry,' Natalie said with belated regret. 'I know I've been a nuisance. Can you tell me about the dam now?'

'I'll tell you over dinner one night.' There was a firm tone to his voice that informed her he would talk when he was ready and right now was not the time. She had the sense to shut up and take pictures, her mind panning the shots from this magnificent road.

'How did you come to work for a Canadian firm?' she asked as he led her back to the vehicle and set off again for the hotel that could now be seen perched on the hillside, surrounded by jungle, looking quite spectacular.

'I joined the firm immediately after I qualified. I've worked for them ever since.'

'So you were here all the time?' She looked at him intently, determined to wheedle out as much information as she could without any dinner.

'Apart from almost one year when I was out of action. I was injured.'

'Were you here during that uprising?' Natalie knew there had been a lot of trouble in Madembi that had coincided with the building of the dam, and she sensed a good story in it. In one way or another, news was in her blood, just as it was in her father's.

'No. I just missed that. After things returned to normal and we set up again, I came out here to take charge. Kane Mallory handed things over to me and went back to Canada. He married my sister, Andrea.'

That stunned her but only for a moment. She looked at him with a great deal of satisfaction. 'Your brother-in-law is the head of Mallory-Carter? Ah!' It was delightful to be able to play the same sort of game with him that he had played with her. Unlike her, though, he didn't rise to the bait, and she knew at once that he had laid this little trap deliberately.

'Now what do I say to that?' he derided. 'Do I get all hot under the collar and assure you that I got where I am on merit and not because of any nepotism?'

'I wasn't about to...' Natalie began hastily, remembering that she would need Kip Forsythe for the next few days at least. He glanced at her scathingly, not at all deceived.

'No? Every chance you get, those little claws are unsheathed, as if you were a small green-eyed black cat, fighting for survival. It must be a hard world you live in, Natalie, even under Daddy's wing.'

'I'm not under his wing. I get no favours and I don't want any. At work I'm just like anyone else—one of the boys. That's how it is.'

'It must be very tricky for the other boys,' he murmured wryly. 'You must have to fight them off. I have a great deal of sympathy for them because even I'm not immune. It's taken a lot of self-restraint to live in the same house for these few days and not devour you. Believe me, I wanted to.'

'Don't think that just because you've been kind I'll let you say anything you like to me!' Natalie looked almost wild-eyed, whipping up anger to cover the other feelings that were rising swiftly to the surface. When he glanced across at her she looked hastily away, hoping that her flushed cheeks showed resentment only.

'I want to make love to you, Natalie. You know that.' His quiet, dark statement seemed to strike right through her, sending shivers up her spine. For a moment her breath stopped. From anyone else it would have been a proposition and she would have dealt with it accordingly. It was unnervingly different from Kip Forsythe— like a statement of fate.

'Don't *talk* like that!' Even to her own ears, her voice sounded frantic. He was making things quite impossible and he must know it. She had never found it possible to flirt. Besides, she loved Neil and she didn't want another man telling her things like that. Even his voice made her shiver. She felt guilty, confused and frighteningly weak.

'Why? Because I'm putting things into words when you would prefer them to be demurely hidden? I was brought up to tell the truth, the whole truth and nothing but the truth, so help me.'

There was laughter there again, back in his voice, and she rounded on him furiously, angry at the wild beating of her own heart.

'Is this how you amuse yourself? Trying to upset me?'

'I'm not trying to upset you, butterfly. I'm merely warning you,' he assured her quietly. 'After all, you're still here and so am I. Circumstances will throw us together. So far, you've been in a slightly pitiful condition, and I did tell you that I was a gentleman of the old school. When you're quite normal and recovered, we'll discuss that affair you mentioned.'

'I'm recovered now, and if you think I'm the sort of person who...'

'I think you're beautiful, desirable and utterly scared. I want you. Here we are.' He swung the Land Rover in between high gates and Natalie decided to keep quiet. It was more dignified and decidedly safer. She had to be cool with Kip but he made it very difficult. When she was acting a part, as she often did to protect herself, Kip managed to see through her and cut the ground away from under her with a few words or even with a look. She found herself adding up the days to her departure in some real agitation.

The Kabala Hotel was luxurious, a showpiece for a country newly emerged into the twentieth century. The great white building was even more impressive at close quarters than it had been from a distance. It had been built with tourists in mind, the surrounding gardens, where crested cranes roamed freely, a colourful array of palms and shrubs, and great lawns stretching to the jungle edge that clothed the sheer drop to the waters of the dam.

The rooms facing the dam had wide balconies and as Natalie stood looking up at the impressive sight two porters raced out to take her luggage. She was very glad. It gave Kip no excuse to come in and no excuse to taunt her further.

'Thank you.' She turned to face him with some reluctance, annoyed with herself to find that she hesitated to raise her eyes to his. Her heart was still thundering away, and even if she could control her voice she couldn't control her eyes.

He was leaning against the Land Rover, looking down at her with the same slight smile on his lips, and he said nothing at all until she was forced to look up at him. This small surrender brought laughter to the back of his dark eyes.

'You're very welcome.' Everything about him mocked her, angered her, and she gave him a stiff half-smile before turning and walking into the hotel, very much aware that he still stood there, his eyes on her intently. It gave her the feeling that she was making an undignified retreat and her natural self-sufficiency tried to reassert itself. She looked round almost defiantly only to find that he was simply grinning widely. She felt like an idiotic child. The less she saw of Kip Forsythe, the better. It was very annoying that he was the one she would have to liaise with on this project.

After a rest and a refreshing shower it was almost time for dinner. Outside the swift African night had descended and Natalie stood on her balcony for a few minutes, breathing in the soft air, watching the lights glitter across the water, following the path of the headlights of cars that occasionally crossed the road over the dam. It was beautiful, even a place to live permanently. There was a sort of excitement in the air, as if something momentous was about to happen. It was an irrational feeling, a feeling quite new to her, as was the wave of guilt that swept over her at the thought of Kip. She went into her room and continued to get ready.

He had no right to intrude into her mind. He had no right to speak as he had done, either. His attitude was very odd as far as she could see because he was not the sort of man who looked as if he would flirt with anyone at all. No doubt he thought she was some idiot and was acting accordingly, amusing himself. If she flirted back he would probably look at her sternly and tell her to behave herself. He had managed with little difficulty to make her feel like a very gauche schoolgirl.

She was still silently fuming as she fastened her earrings and stood back to survey the final effect. Her dress was a soft swirl of organza over satin, the colours muted orange, brown and green. The gold chains she loved looked good with it and now her earrings flashed in the lamplight, swinging from her ears beside the blue-black of her long hair. In high-heeled gold sandals she was slender, tall and very aloof-looking, exactly what she wanted to be. Any of her inner problems remained hidden as usual and she went down to dinner with no thought of conversation with other guests in her mind.

Almost the first person she saw was Kip. She was hit again by the choking feeling of alarm and she wanted to turn back to her room but it was too late; he had already seen her. Resplendent and handsome in white dinner-jacket, he came walking slowly towards her, quite spoiling the feeling she had of being tall and aloof because even before he reached her she began to feel small and agitated.

He panicked her, more every time she saw him, and she had never seen him dressed like this before. The impression of a tough, sardonic film star was overwhelming.

'Good evening, Natalie. Join us for a drink in the bar.'

In the process of staring at him almost open-mouthed she nearly missed the 'us' bit. Not for long; his partner came forward very determinedly and Natalie saw that he was not short of female companionship after all. The woman with him was much more than a companion as far as Natalie could see, and she claimed his arm with a certain determination that had more to do with possession than friendliness.

'Oh, Annette. This is Natalie West.' Kip looked across at Natalie. 'Annette Shelton. Like me, Annette works out here.'

And that's not all she does, Natalie found herself thinking, quite cattily, forcing herself to smile at the other woman. A blonde, she was blue-eyed, well-groomed, good-looking but not beautiful, bossy and sexy, Natalie catalogued in her mind. She wondered how many nights Kip Forsythe had been 'in love' with Annette.

'What will you drink, Natalie?' Belatedly she glanced back at Kip. Damn him! Why were his eyes always smiling like that? Why did he worry her? It was impossible to tell what he was thinking. She had never met anyone like him before. Tall, bronzed, golden, his fair hair gleaming, he was one of a kind, an original.

'Natalie?'

'Er—I'll have a dry sherry.' His dark brows raised at her blushes but he said nothing although she had the nasty feeling he had been reading her mind.

The drinks had just been served when Natalie was called to the foyer. Her hire car had arrived and she was glad of the excuse to leave the happy couple. To her chagrin, Kip strolled out as she was taking delivery of the car and began to walk around it, inspecting it, throwing questions at the European driver who turned out to be the owner of the hire firm.

'Let's have the bonnet up, Bill,' he ordered, ignoring Natalie's outraged expression.

'This car's in good shape, Kip, but I'll oblige.' They both peered under the bonnet as Natalie stood feeling extremely superfluous and greatly irritated.

'Run the engine,' Kip ordered, and it was the beginning of a steady, scrupulous inspection that had Natalie fuming, her rage barely contained when Kip agreed that it was 'probably passable'.

'Do you find it impossible to mind your own business?' As the man left she grabbed the keys and pushed them into her bag, glaring up at Kip in the lights.

'I'm an engineer. Things mechanical fascinate me.'

'You're not that sort of an engineer!'

'For your information, I can strip a car down to the last nut and bolt and put it all back together again.'

Natalie noticed he had brought Annette in his car, the one he had driven her from the airport in. It was gleaming under the lights. *She* had been brought to the hotel in a dusty Land Rover! It made her more annoyed than ever.

'Then strip your own car down and leave mine alone.'

He looked down at her, taking her arm when she would have stormed back inside. 'I've got the hang of you now, Natalie,' he warned softly, his dark eyes on her angry face. 'If you take off into the bush and break down, somebody will have to rescue you and that somebody would have to be me. You'll never ask for help and you'll never say where you're going, so I have to be quite sure that you're reasonably safe.'

'I've been taking care of myself for years!' Natalie snapped, her anger covering her embarrassment. She would not ask for his help, it was true, because he had too much of an effect on her, an unsteadying effect, and she wanted nothing to do with him at all. He was quiet, smiling danger.

'And have you been taking care of yourself well?' He looked at her seriously. 'An angry little cat, with eyes like emeralds. Calm yourself. A few days and we'll be far from each other, no need whatever to meet again for the rest of our lives.'

'Good! I live for that moment.' She walked in and he followed. She had no intention of collecting her drink and staying to have some social chat but Kip had already made plans and that was clear as the head waiter came up with smiling deference.

'Your table is ready, Mr Forsythe. I've placed Miss West with you.'

'Thank you.' His hand came tightly to Natalie's arm, stilling her rising denial. 'Surely you don't imagine I'll allow you to sit all alone when I'm dining here?'

'You have a dinner companion already,' Natalie reminded him crossly. He had her trapped again, fluttery inside at the idea of spending an evening facing him.

'I'm prepared to act as escort to two ladies. Behave yourself, Natalie; we're not at home now.'

'Look——!' she began, snatching her arm from his grasp but he collected her again immediately, his cool fingers sending warning thrills right through her.

'I promise not to tell any tales,' he murmured against her ear, as Annette Shelton walked out of the bar looking decidedly miffed. 'There's no need for Annette to know how delicious you look in a white towel.'

His thumb was stroking in small circles against the skin of her arm and for the moment Natalie admitted defeat. Those few words had brought back the shivering excitement of Kip's dark eyes burning over her. Annette's bright blue eyes were attempting to maim her and she felt definitely outnumbered.

'You're with a television company?' Annette asked as they settled down to their meal. 'I suppose you pry into things a lot?'

'Only in a very nice way.' Recognising a battle in the offing, Natalie was prepared to back-pedal. It was nothing to her if this woman was jealous and she certainly was not about to be drawn into it. 'Most of our work is in making documentaries. That's why I'm here now.'

'Yes. Kip *did* tell me. You must be glad to be at the hotel at last. It must have been awful finding yourself ill all this way from England and having to lean on Kip's good nature. If only he'd told me, I would have been there to help.'

'Mina helped,' Kip put in speedily as he saw Natalie's green eyes flash sparks. 'I didn't exactly have to act as a lady's maid.'

Only when he had undressed her and lifted her into bed. He didn't need to mention it. The memory was all in those dark eyes and Natalie's face flushed at his steady gaze. Annette looked more suspicious than ever.

'Well, that's a relief, darling,' she murmured, her hand stroking his arm. 'I did wonder why I wasn't seeing as much of you as usual.'

'Things will be back to normal in a few days,' Natalie assured her quickly. 'Being ill has delayed things and now I'll really have to put a spurt on. My team are due out here as soon as possible and I'm supposed to have everything ready for them.'

'Are you going to interview local celebrities?' The other woman perked up somewhat.

'Annette asks because she's in that category herself, being head of the new secondary school out here,' Kip enlightened her wryly.

So that was where she got her bossy air? Natalie looked interested and Annette softened at the thought of television, herself in the bright eye of the camera.

'Tell me about it.' Natalie leaned forward with every appearance of keenness, completely in her element. She switched on the small, powerful recorder she invariably kept in her bag. Not much bigger than a powder compact, it could pick up sound over a good range, certainly from across the table. Normally she held it openly in her hand but now she placed it surreptitiously on her lap. This was where Kip Forsythe found out that she *did* know her business. Perhaps after this he would back off and leave her to get on alone?

Annette waxed eloquent. Natalie watched with wide, awe-stricken green eyes and the tape recorder turned silently. There were a few times during this boastful monologue when she feared that Kip would intervene and bring it to an end. He looked bored out of his mind and Natalie found it necessary to glance at him occasionally with entrancing jewelled eyes until finally he just let Annette talk as he settled to watching Natalie's beautiful face.

'That was really interesting,' Natalie assured Annette as she finally ran down, her face flushed with effort and wine. 'I may get the camera over to your school. Of course, our project here is the dam itself, but the school seems to represent progress. In any case, I do quite a few articles for newspapers on a freelance basis and after the production is launched they'll be very keen I imagine. You'll certainly be in an article.' She lifted the recorder to the table and switched it off with a certain amount of flourish. 'I'll even transcribe this tonight. It was fascinating.'

The effect was electric. Annette blushed angrily, memory of her open boasting coming to her belatedly, and for the first time ever Natalie saw real rage on Kip's face.

'You were taping me?' Annette almost choked over the words and Natalie gave her a sweet smile.

'Oh, I always tape my interviews. My shorthand is not too good.'

'It wasn't an interview!'

'But I distinctly remember you asking if I was going to interview local celebrities and Kip said you were one yourself. You *did* know that I'm part of the media.'

'I never expected this! It's downright underhand to hide a tape recorder!'

'Not at all,' Natalie said breezily, standing and gathering her things. 'The sight of it puts people off. They don't say any of the things they would say normally. I'll let you have a copy, of course, when I've got it typed up.' She murmured her thanks and bowed out gracefully. Kip stood but he said nothing at all and this time the dark eyes were anything but warm and smiling. She felt she had stood on the tail of a tiger who was not quite prepared to bite.

He bit sooner than she had anticipated. There was a knock on her door almost as soon as she had entered her room and, thinking it was a maid, she opened it at once. Kip stood outside looking extremely forbidding and it was clear that at this moment she was not at all an exotic butterfly but a very disreputable member of the television world.

'What can I do for you?' Natalie looked up at him and tried very hard to outface him, with no success at all.

'You can wipe that tape.' He stepped into the room and closed the door, standing tall and rather intimidating, leaning against it.

'Are you mad? This is what I do for a living.'

'No. This is what you do for spite,' he corrected frostily. 'You invited Annette to make a fool of herself.'

'And she obliged very nicely. If you're worried about her, keep her out of my path. What have you done with her, sent her home alone or settled her with a double brandy?'

'She's in the bar. I'll take her home when I've dealt with you. I don't think a double brandy will restore her temper but it's not *that* you have to worry about.'

'I'm not worried at all.' Natalie tossed her black hair back and moved away, gasping when he jerked her back towards him.

'Perhaps you should be, television lady. Annette can take care of herself but you know damned well why I kept silent and listened to that boring talk. I was too allured by those green-eyed glances I kept getting to intervene. Make a fool of anyone you like and good luck to you. Make a fool of me and take what's coming to you.'

"I don't know what you mean!" Natalie suddenly realised that he was not in any way as she had known him. He was furious, boiling with a silent rage that altered him completely. He was not now a man to challenge. He was all cold power. He had allowed himself to be beguiled by her glances and she had done it deliberately. He was in no doubt about that. Audacity left her and only alarm remained.

His hands left her shoulders and gripped her slender waist, pulling her to him with one angry movement.

'Then I'll show you. Look at me with bedroom eyes and this is where you'll find me—in your bedroom.'

One arm lashed round her waist, his free hand tangling in her long hair as he forced her face up to his and took her lips stormily. There was not the sweet possession there had been before. This was savage, cruel, a bitter punishment. This was another man and she whimpered under the fierce pressure of his lips.

It did not make him relent. He was intent on punishment, incensed at her trick to keep him silent as Annette talked. He pulled her harshly against him until her hips were grinding into his, until the whole hard length of his body seemed to be indelibly printed against her softness.

'Please!' She managed to free her lips and for one frightening moment he looked as if he would continue the hostile chastisement. His body did not relax and his hands held her tightly to him, his dark eyes burning into hers.

'Don't ever tease me again, Natalie,' he said heavily at last, his glance skimming her bruised lips. 'This is not the way I want to crush you. The next time you're in my arms you'll be there willingly.'

'I won't be,' she whispered. 'I'll be gone almost before you know it.'

'I'll know it,' he assured her ominously, 'because by that time you'll belong to me, even if it's only once.'

'No! You have no right to talk like that.' She pushed frantically against his chest, her heart beating with wild dismay as she felt the surge of arousal that hardened his body against hers.

'Give me the right,' he said huskily.

His lips brushed her neck, his hand now teasing against her vulnerable nape, the cruelty gone, the powerful, intoxicating sweetness back, and excitement surged through her as his touch banished fear. His eyes looked into hers, the deep brown darkened to near black, his pupils enlarged, glazed, and she knew just how much he wanted her.

Her breasts tightened and thrust forward, her own body betraying her, and his voice was almost slurred as he breathed her name.

'Natalie!'

She tried to ignore him, to remain aloof, but it was impossible. The chemistry was too strong. The hands that had attempted to hold him off now slid around his neck and he drew her between his parted legs, sensuously pressing her close, his hand moving down her spine, moulding her to his body.

There was no outrage in her at all at this possessive display of sexual need. It was raging between them like a fire out of control and she knew that her own soft body was accepting the hard thrust of his desire in a way she would never be able to deny. It was madness. He was nothing to her at all. She didn't want him to be anything. She hardly knew him and yet her arms were around his neck, clinging willingly, her mouth open under his, eagerly permitting the invasion of his tongue.

She moaned softly and his lips left hers to trail down her slender neck, his arms rocking her against him.

'Come back home with me, Natalie,' he groaned. 'You want me, too.'

'No!' She shook her head frantically, hanging on to sanity but only just, and his hand captured her black hair, tightening it around his wrist like a shining rope as the tip of his tongue circled her lips.

'No, you won't come, or no, you don't want me?' he asked thickly.

'I'm here to work. I hardly know you. I don't *want* to know you!'

He looked into her frantic eyes, his own too burningly dark to be smiling. 'You know me. Your body recognises me. It recognised me the very first time I touched you. You want me. In our minds, we're lovers, Natalie.'

'No!' She stepped free on trembling legs, moving from the tempting awareness, wanting to be back as soon as she had moved. 'I know exactly what I'm going to do. I always know. Didn't tonight teach you anything? I work in television and I'll get things in any way I can.'

She could hear the shrill sound of her own voice. She was panicking, hoping childishly that words of denial would free her from her own desire.

'Even if it means teasing me?'

'Yes.' She managed to say it but she couldn't look at him.

'And what were you gaining by clinging to me just now?' The dark voice seemed to brush against her like a live wire, shivering along her spine. She had no answer and he knew it.

'Leave me alone,' she snapped desperately, turning completely away. 'I'm here to do a job. If I can manage without you I will. When the team arrives, one of the men can deal with you all the time.'

'Oh, no, they can't, Natalie,' he assured her quietly. 'I'll deal with you and nobody else. I want to look into those green eyes and see them tell me to my face what they dare not tell me now.'

'Then we'll do the documentary without you.'

She made herself turn to face him, determined to put a stop to this at once but he was not there. As quietly as he had come in, he had left, and Natalie leaned against the door, frantically denying what her body assured her was true. She wanted Kip as she had never ever wanted any other man. She had never even considered giving herself to anyone, not even to Neil, but a few moments more with Kip and she would have been incapable of moving out of his arms.

It was not love. She knew that. It was powerful, though, too powerful to be resisted, and the only way to escape was to be as far away from him as possible. She wanted Neil to come with an almost frenzied longing. He wasn't hers but he would restore her sanity. Just to see him would calm her. She wanted her own people around her, familiarity to ward off a devastating sexual attraction that threatened to set her on fire.

There was a message from the minister the next morning, a kindly, courteous letter delivered by hand as Natalie ate breakfast on her veranda. Gabriel Basoni, the minister of culture, would be greatly honoured if she would call at his office at ten-thirty today and discuss the project with him. He would then be delighted to offer her lunch. It was just the sort of boost to her confidence that Natalie needed and she got ready with great pleasure, marshalling her father's plans, her own ideas and her rough notes.

As she drove the miles into the city, along quite good roads, she admitted that part of her satisfaction with this turn of events was because she was moving out of

Kip's sphere. If she could get the minister himself to co-operate then it would be possible to cut Kip's part in the production down to a minimum. He was an unnecessary complication in her life and she was more than horrified at her own response to him.

He had pushed Neil right to the back of her mind and she couldn't really afford that, because when she saw Neil again she knew she was going to be very vulnerable. The weeks since their break-up had been a time of inner battle with herself and that battle had to go on. How could she be prepared for him when Kip was constantly taking her mind away from her own fight? She almost felt guilty instead of relieved to realise that there was now no hurt when she thought of Neil. Was there something wrong with her emotions? Could she simply stop loving someone because another man excited her sexually? If she could, then she really did have a problem.

CHAPTER FIVE

THE government offices were in the capital city, ten miles away, and Natalie arrived early. This was not yet on a par with Nairobi, even if it ever would be, but there were some fine old buildings—a left-over from colonial days—and the ministry of culture was housed in one of these. She was shown into the minister's office at once, glad that he was not yet there as she took a few moments to compose herself and look around at the quite splendid room.

It had every appearance of being the workplace of a man who liked a civilised way of life. There were good pictures on the walls, expensive easy chairs and a very impressive desk that held photographs of two small children and a very pretty woman whom Natalie took to be the minister's wife.

He came in as she was leaning across to get a better look at the photographs and Natalie almost sighed aloud with relief as she looked up into a smiling African face. He must be in his late thirties, handsome, easygoing, educated and very well dressed. This was a kind man. She took to him on sight, the humour at the back of his eyes making her relax.

'At last, Miss West!' He walked across and shook hands as she stood. 'I trust you are now recovered from your virus? A most unfortunate introduction to my country.'

He motioned her to a seat and settled behind his desk, looking hard at her for a minute as she straightened her skirt and rested back against the dark leather. This morning she had decided to wear the one suit she had brought with her, a silk, slim-fitting creation in a rich deep mulberry. It showed off her black hair even more and her eyes looked startlingly green. The minister noticed.

'You must forgive my staring,' he said apologetically. 'Your colouring amazes me. To me, black hair has dark eyes. Your eyes are such an astonishing green that I expect any moment to find that I am dreaming.'

'My mother had green eyes,' Natalie explained with a smile. 'She had red hair.'

'Extraordinary!' His glance rested lovingly on his own two children and his wife and Natalie thought what a wonderful father he must be. She settled down to really liking Gabriel Basoni.

By lunchtime he had approved all her plans, explained to her the ceremony that would take place for the official opening of the Kabala Dam and talked enthusiastically about the future of Madembi. Her little tape recorder was on the desk in front of him but after a second they both forgot all about it. He was a pleasure to talk to.

They were still discussing Natalie's idea of a series of freelance articles on Madembi as they went to lunch in a chauffeur-driven car with the Madembi coat of arms on the door. It had been a most pleasant morning, culminating in their being bowed regally to their table in the very best hotel that the capital offered.

'I will tell your other guest you have arrived, Minister,' the head waiter offered and Natalie stiffened with apprehension, pleasure going swiftly away as a few seconds later Kip walked into the dining-room to be greeted as an old friend by Gabriel Basoni.

'Natalie.' Kip gave her a polite nod as he took his seat, his eyes flaring over her, and she found her face flushing uncomfortably as the memory of the previous evening came rushing back. She only had to look into his eyes and she could feel herself pressed against him. The chemistry was so strong that she wanted to jump up and rush out like a flustered schoolgirl. He was in a light-weight suit, darkly sophisticated against his pale shirt and dark tie. The thick, fair hair looked almost unreal and she had to tear her eyes away from him.

'It is fortunate that you know each other so well,' the minister said with satisfaction. 'It will be easier to work together. So you see, my dear Kip, getting you to bring Miss West from Nairobi was a very good idea.'

'Though a trifle devious,' Kip murmured wryly.

'I'm a diplomat! What do you expect?'

The very way they talked to each other told Natalie that these two were close friends and that getting out of dealing with Kip on this production would be almost impossible, in spite of her threats of the previous night.

'As you are already friends. I can safely leave things to you both from now on,' the minister said happily. 'I greatly approve of Miss West's plans and she knows her business well.'

'She's a tough television lady,' Kip put in drily, and Gabriel Basoni looked at him askance.

'Surely not tough. She had treated me very gently; even her tape recorder did not intrude.'

Kip's dark eyes slid to Natalie's suddenly apprehensive face. If he said anything about last night's dinner she would face a great deal of embarrassment. 'You use a tape recorder, Natalie? That should be useful. Keep it out of sight though when you're recording me. I might get anxious with stage-fright.'

A very subtle rebuff. Natalie risked a glare at him but he simply smiled right into her eyes and the minister settled down to enjoying his lunch. He had interviewed Natalie, given his own interview, brought the two interested parties together and very gently issued an order. She would work with Kip. Kip's amused dark eyes recognised her predicament and she was very pleased to be able to walk off and leave him as they returned to the official car. By the time he left the city she would be back at the hotel if she could manage it. She would contact him only when it was absolutely necessary, preferably with every other member of her team there.

At first it was easy. Kip made no attempt to contact her and she had her own transport. She planned the film meticulously, wandered around the town until she was quite well known, people willing to stop and smile into her camera as she took her shots. Factories were going up, housing being built, and already the cables that would carry the power for prosperity stretched out of sight on high pylons that strode like giants into the distance.

It was all coming together beautifully, the shots, the sounds, the script growing under her hands. Many nights she ate dinner in her room and worked and gradually the alarming excitement of Kip's touch faded into a dream. She would deal with the dam itself when she felt more sure but it could not be put off much longer and for that she would need Kip.

She gave herself one more day. During her chats with local people she had been told of the falls that were hidden high in the jungle-clad hills. The Tamberi Falls marked the point where the Kabala River dropped from a higher plateau and it would make a good camera shot if they could get up to it. Natalie had to find out and then she would send for the team because time was running out fast.

She set off early and the people at the hotel were quite prepared to make up a packed lunch for her and provide a map. The road was good, she was told, and she started out with plenty of film and high hopes for a successful day.

At first the road *was* good and with the car windows wound down, her sunglasses protecting her from the bright glare, Natalie enjoyed her adventure. It was nothing new for her to take off across some unknown country, breaking ground for the camera and the production team, and this seemed quite normal.

It was only after an hour, when the metalled road disappeared and the familiar pot-holed red earth track became her highway, that Natalie had misgivings. The jungle now seemed closer, the trees higher, and she kept an eye on the side of the road with increasing anxiety.

The air was almost burningly hot, still and heavy, the humidity making her breathless, and she longed to stop and get out of the car. She had more sense than that, however. Since leaving the metalled road she had seen no other car and this part of the country looked altogether wild. Wild country held wild animals and she found her eyes darting into the thickening trees with increasing frequency.

Natalie was almost ready to turn back and give up the idea altogether when she heard the sound she had subconsciously been waiting for, the great thunder of rushing, falling water. Around the next bend the trees miraculously fell away, the area almost returning to scrub land. There was a huge basin that looked at least a mile across and through this the great river rushed in a torrent.

Looking up she saw the high land above her, sparsely clad with trees and over the top the Tamberi Falls leapt into the air and fell to the river below, wild, white water that filled the air with thunder, crashing over huge rocks, glittering like cascading diamonds, the rumble and roar of plummeting water reverberating around the huge natural basin.

It was perhaps the most dramatic scene she had ever witnessed in her life, grandeur that took her breath away. Its size was staggering and had she been with a companion it would have been impossible to hold a conversation. Even the noise was on a magnificent scale.

She was too close. She realised that at once and she looked round impatiently to find a spot where the camera could do justice to this striking scene. Fortunately the basin stretched for some way and, turning, she drove slowly back until she could turn from the road and drive across rough ground to the edge of the river.

Here, there was an astonishing haven of tranquillity. The river seemed to spare a moment to recover from the shock of the falling water; it swirled in to the bank, rippling across shingle and red earth, crystal clear and dazzling in the sun. From the bank she could turn and take shots of the falls in peace because now the noise was less intense.

She settled to her task, ignoring the heat and her thirst, promising herself a drink when she had finished, promising herself too the luxury of a few moments dabbling her feet in the clear water. She was utterly absorbed, spellbound, her face filled with the excitement of the shots, her mind seeing the television camera's final scanning of this. Perspiration slid down her face but she ignored it, finally sighing with satisfaction and turning back to the car for her drink and packed lunch, the whole thing more than worth the effort.

The sight that met her eyes as she turned chilled her even in the heat. The car was axle deep in the earth. What she had taken to be the hard sunbaked earth of a river bank was in fact some sort of quicksand, not unusual in this sort of terrain. It was not deep and dangerous but the weight of the car had been enough to activate the slow drag down.

The danger was all too real. It was the danger of being here alone, a few sandwiches, a soft drink and then what? Natalie remembered the last part of her drive, the narrow track, the enclosing jungle. She would have to walk back, risking anything she might face en route. Kip had made sure that her car was mechanically sound. He hadn't reckoned on sheer stupidity. Nobody would look for her until much later, in fact, she might not even be missed until morning. For days she had been wandering around until late evening, often eating in her room. The people at the hotel were quite accustomed to her odd hours.

Natalie opened the car door and sat disconsolately on the seat, her eyes staring unseeingly at the river and the mighty falls, her feet out of the car. She jumped up and moved hastily as the soft earth began to drag stealthily at her feet, already submerging the soles of her track shoes.

She sprang away from the car and turned on harder ground to see that it had sunk even further. One thing was sure. She couldn't lock herself inside it as evening came and sit it out hoping to be rescued. She would never sleep because now she had no idea how deep the quicksand went.

She was staring at the car, her face slick with perspiration, her shirt sticking to her back, when unbelievably she heard the sound of an approaching vehicle. For a minute she was dazed and then she ran out to the track, waving her arms frantically, a *frisson* of unease sliding over her when she saw a Land Rover coming at speed and recognised the furious driver.

Kip stopped right beside her and she could see that rage was beating inside him as he sprang out and bore down on her with an air of menace that almost had her backing off.

'You stupid little fool! You're no more capable of looking after yourself than a disobedient child!' He grabbed her arms and yanked her forward, ignoring her distress. 'Have you no more sense than to come up here alone? Do you imagine I've got nothing better to do with my time than to chase all over keeping an eye on you?'

He looked as if he was going to shake her and she was so upset that she wouldn't have resisted if he had. He seemed to get a grip on himself though and let her go, turning away in disgust.

'Get in your car and drive back. I'll escort you to the hotel.'

'I—I can't.'

He spun round furiously to glare at her but his eyes followed hers as she stared disconsolately at the car, now well and truly wedged in the soft earth of the river bank. For a second he swore under his breath until she thought the air might turn blue and he was not amused when she interrupted.

'I—I know you're not too pleased to have to give me a lift back...'

'A lift back?' His eyes narrowed to dark slits. 'Do you realise what would have happened if I hadn't just chanced to call into the hotel? You could have been here all night or at least until someone there decided to raise the alarm. Or did you plan to hike back nonchalantly?' he added with great suspicion.

'I hadn't decided. I never expected to find the car stuck.'

Natalie's lips began to tremble even though she tried hard to stop them. She was shaking for quite a lot of reasons. It had given her a nasty shock to see her only means of transport so firmly stuck and Kip's arrival had not lessened the tension because he was both furious and insulting. Any more and she would burst into tears.

'Get in the Land Rover,' he snapped, turning away from this sign of weak femininity, but she wavered even then.

'I'm thirsty. I've got a drink in the car and anyway, my bag and my camera...'

'I'll get them!' He strode off but she followed dejectedly, trailing along behind him like a whipped dog. It pleased him not at all. He glowered at her and handed her the drink, watching as she drank it greedily.

'I'll have to rinse my face. I'm too hot.'

The river looked cool and inviting, the shallows no threat, and she stepped towards the edge of the bank, giving a little shriek of alarm as Kip grabbed her and forcibly jerked her back.

'Have you been in that water?'

She was so surprised that she just stared at him, her body beginning to tremble more than ever.

'*Have* you?'

'N-no. I was going to paddle after I'd had a drink but before I could you came and...'

He gave a great sigh of relief, the sudden tension easing from his face, but there was nothing kindly about the scowl he directed at her.

'*Never* go near fresh water in this part of the world!' he rasped, his hand biting into her arm. 'There's a disease in the water that's all too easy to catch. It's not even safe to be too near the falls because of the spray.' He suddenly seemed to see how scared he had made her and he turned her back to the track. 'I've got something to rinse your face,' he muttered.

He took a large jerry can from the back of the Land Rover and began to unscrew the cap.

'What is it?'

'Well, it's not petrol,' he snapped, taking a large white handkerchief from his pocket and pouring water over it. 'Here. Rinse your face.'

It was delightfully cool and she held the handkerchief out for more, feeling a little like Oliver Twist as he regarded her with raised eyebrows.

'Can—can you pour a bit on my face?' she almost begged. He did. She closed her eyes and felt the blissful cool liquid wash over her face and the front of her hair, opening her eyes when he suddenly stopped.

He was looking at her intently, his gaze intensifying as she licked the drops from her lips in an unknowingly erotic gesture.

'Thank you. That was wonderful.' She smiled up at him, not at all realising why he was so suddenly silent, the rage gone. It was only as she felt the blouse sticking to her that she appreciated just how she looked. The water had poured on more than her face. Her blouse was soaked, her breasts clearly visible through the thin material, their dark nipples pressed sharply forward.

'Get inside,' he said abruptly. 'We don't exactly want to drown you—not yet at any rate.'

Natalie was all too keen to get inside. Her relief at being rescued now churning up inside with other feelings and as he got in beside her and started the vehicle she kept her eyes firmly turned away, praying she would dry out with great speed.

'Did you get your shots?' He spoke after a few minutes in a voice so controlled that she felt even more wary.

'Yes.' She hesitated and then added, 'I'm sorry I went off like that. It was stupid. You're quite right.'

'You scared the living daylights out of me. I think I've gone grey.' His voice was curiously husky, showing more emotion than she had ever heard, and she turned to look at him.

'I'm not your responsibility, Kip.' She suddenly had a great desire to treat him gently, which was not at all how she usually felt. It was safe now that Kip was here. If they met a wild animal he would probably get out and order it off the path. She gave a little giggle at the very idea and he glanced across.

'I hope you're not going to go all hysterical on me now.'

'No. I was just thinking.'

'So long as you're not planning I'll feel fairly safe.' He went very quiet and after a few seconds she closed her eyes, surprised when as she was almost dozing off he pulled over to the side of the road and stopped the engine.

'What happened?' Natalie opened sleepy eyes and looked at him, puzzled to find him sitting with his arms across the wheel, looking out along the road.

'Nothing at all. I'm recovering from a violent reaction before I reach civilisation. Right at this moment I don't know how I'd cope with oncoming vehicles. I imagined you were asleep.'

'There was no need to react so violently,' she assured him quietly. 'I would have been perfectly safe.'

'Oh? You had a foolproof plan?' His voice was back to harsh derision as he glanced across at her but he looked away quickly as his eyes seemed to be drawn to the still-wet blouse.

'No. I'd only just found out that...' In spite of her desire to be aloof and sure of herself, her voice suddenly trembled. 'I was scared.'

He looked back at her sharply as he heard the fear still lingering.

'So you're not as tough as you think you are?'

Natalie shook her head, trying to cope with her own reaction, rather horrified to find a stray tear trailing down her cheek.

'Oh, for God's sake, stop that!' He almost shouted at her and then when she looked at him in dismay he reached for her, wrapping his arms around her and pulling her close. 'Stop crying, Natalie. You're wet enough as it is.'

He rubbed his cheek against her hair and she looked up at him rather woefully.

'I had a shock and then you came—shouting. You scared me.'

'Not as much as you scared me.' His arms tightened. 'That place is almost virgin jungle. The falls have not yet attained the status of a tourist attraction. Apart from the animals that go down to that very spot to drink, there are snakes—plenty of them.'

'You don't have to frighten me any more,' she assured him shakily, submitting to a great urge and burying her face against his shoulder.

'So what do I have to do instead?' His lips skimmed her cheek, making her lift her head back, her throat still glistening with the water, and he bent his fair head, his tongue sensuously licking her skin, collecting the moisture from the slender arch of her throat until she gave a low murmur and melted towards him, lifting her face to meet the burning pressure of his lips as his mouth opened over hers.

'Do you still want to pretend there's nothing between us?' His voice was smouldering and when he lifted his head and looked into her dazed eyes, the green darkening with every passing heartbeat, Natalie shook her head slowly. She could hardly pretend. Every time he touched her she lit up inside. Though his mouth was no longer on hers she still felt the burning imprint; blood seemed to be rushing in her ears, making the whole world rock unsteadily.

Every nerve in her body was flaring, the longing to be kissed again almost unbearable. It was right there in her eyes and he made a low sound of satisfaction, a growl deep in his throat, and began to kiss her parted lips again, hungrily and drowsily.

'What do you propose to do about this?'

His question came against her skin as his mouth nuzzled her neck sensuously, his hand lifting her hair away from her satin skin.

'I—I...nothing...'

'Nothing?' He bit into her neck at the point where it met her smooth shoulder and it was not a particularly gentle bite. It was slow, erotic, possessive, with just enough force to make her cry out. Shivers ran down her spine, spreading out all over her skin and she gasped as his teeth closed gently on her flesh again.

'Kip!'

'What, my beautiful? You think I'd hurt you?' He kissed the hollow of her neck, his tongue against the frantic pulse, his mouth closing over hers again as she gave a low moan and abandoned herself to sensation.

It was an explosion of feeling, a conflagration of brilliant excitement that sent thrills to every part of her. From the very centre of her being ripples rushed out to engulf her.

Her name was a low and repeated sound on his lips as he kissed each part of her face, her neck, her hair. His hands burned into her, searching her narrow waist and slender flanks with a growing demand that Natalie knew would not be denied for very much longer. She had no will to break away. Kip's urgency was part of her too.

Tasting was no longer enough. They strained together with a frantic yearning and her body moved to accommodate him when his hand slid inside her shirt to close around the still-damp contours of her breast, his fingers seeking the sharply aroused peak with an almost cruel compulsion.

'I want you! I can't wait for you!' He breathed the words into her mouth, arching her back, the close confines of the seat bringing a low growl of impatience to his throat. 'I can't make love to you here, in the front seat of a car on an open road. Come back home with me. Stay with me, Natalie!'

'I can't!' The denial seemed to be torn out of her. Words seemed to bring her to her senses and she found herself looking with distressed eyes into the burning dark of his. His skin was flushed and the fingers that flexed against her breast trembled.

'Can't, or won't?' he asked thickly. 'You want to be in my bed and I want you there.' He sat up, moving slowly away from her, relaxing the vibrant sexual tension.

'Please!' She tried to sit upright, trembling too much to really trust her own voice, looking quickly away. 'This—this is just one of those things it's...' What was it? He didn't love her, she didn't love him. It was merely a sexual need, the sort of thing that had always disgusted her. It was an almost violent feeling that she could not accept and yet there was nothing of disgust in her when she thought of being in Kip's arms.

She found herself meeting his eyes almost warily and for a second his darkened gaze held hers.

'It's sheer necessity—for both of us,' he informed her in an uneven voice. 'You want me to promise it won't happen again? I can't guarantee it. I don't want to. I'm through pretending, Natalie. I want you as I've wanted no woman before in my life.'

He started the engine and she slowly allowed herself to breathe again. Nobody had ever taken her by storm before. Nobody had ever said outright the things that Kip had said. Her own reaction to him scared her and she knew his idea of love—one or two nights. She looked out of the window, trying to compose herself and not doing very well at all.

'How long do you imagine we can keep this up?' he growled as they neared her hotel. Neither of them had spoken all the way in and the tension had mounted with every passing mile. 'I'm not letting you out of my sight because you'll surely kill yourself as you could so easily have done today. When you're in my sight I want you and you melt into me as soon as I touch you. You want exactly what I want, Natalie. Admit it.'

'I—I don't. I can't think why...' She heard her own voice shaking and he certainly heard it too. 'When the others come—— '

'There'll just be more people around to get in the way,' he snapped. 'Crowds won't make any difference, however large.'

'You forget. I'll be leaving with them.'

He shot her one of those lightning glances that brought shudders to her skin.

'All right, butterfly. Escape. Forget me.'

'I will,' she said angrily, annoyed at the sudden taunting note in his voice. 'In any case, there's nothing to forget. I don't even know you at all.'

'You knew me on sight,' he scoffed.

'You didn't even *like* me on sight!'

Unexpectedly he grinned to himself. 'You seemed inadequate for your profession. I knew as soon as I saw you just who would be looking after you. It annoyed me. I've had to rescue you with almost every move you made.'

'I'm really sorry,' Natalie fumed bitterly, glad to have the excuse for temper. It was more reassuring than her other feelings.

'Don't be,' he interrupted before she could enlarge on her sarcastic beginning. 'I'm getting a taste for tucking you under my arm. You're different. Maybe I've grown too accustomed to women who cope with events and stand up to them.'

'Or lie down for them,' Natalie put in with a crude annoyance, thinking of Annette Shelton.

'I confessed my love-life,' he murmured infuriatingly, just as she realised that the thought of Annette Shelton made her feel jealous. What was she thinking of? Jealous? She had been jealous of Paula because of Neil. Kip Forsythe could go and do whatever he liked. In about a week she would be away from here and never see him again.

They stopped at the hotel and as usual he defeated her by being himself.

'Don't fight, baby,' he murmured softly, shocking her by his use of the endearment. She looked at him a little wildly, stunned to feel all her antagonism fading. That devilish smile was back in his eyes again, his passion controlled, and Natalie just sat looking at him when she knew perfectly well she should be getting out and storming off inside.

He trailed one long brown finger across her cheek, touching her lips gently as he reached them, his gaze fastened on their softness.

'You think I'll hurt you, don't you?'

'Yes.' She confessed it because she suddenly felt that he could and the stunned expression in her eyes had the smile reaching his lips.

'You're quite wrong,' he assured her quietly, opening the door and letting her out. She dared not look back and as she went inside she heard him pull away.

It left her in a sort of dream state. She hardly knew the face that looked back at her as she stared in the mirror. Affairs had never been her idea of how to live her life and yet when Kip touched her she seemed to forget all her own rules.

She showered and then sat looking out over the dam. She was here to work and so far she had done a lot of that in spite of her bad beginning. She collected her notes and looked at the picture that was emerging. She had a fairly comprehensive plan worked out and as far as she could see the team should now arrive. It would bring Neil and Paula and a considerable amount of heartache but it would bring safety. She telephoned her father. He was both delighted and relieved. The others would be there in two days.

She was just wondering about her photographs when Kip rang. Just the sound of his deep voice had her clutching the telephone tightly but he was quiet, nothing but friendly.

'If I make a reservation at the hotel for tonight, will you have dinner with me?'

It was unexpected and for a second Natalie didn't answer, stunned by her own feelings. She wanted to see him. Just the sound of his voice excited her. Would she have to face another evening sitting opposite Kip and Annette Shelton? Was that what he had in mind? And what about later? Would he be content to simply say goodnight and go? Everything inside her seemed to be in a ferment as she struggled with feelings she had never faced before.

As a girl she had never seemed to go through the normal exciting encounters of her friends, in spite of her beauty. She had been too serious and, on top of that, her father had always been a rather alarmingly powerful man, scaring would-be boyfriends off with one sharp glance, even though it was mostly by accident.

Her feelings for Neil had been a calm and enduring affection that had grown. A comfortable thing. Now she was confused by her own emotions, by the fluttering inside. Kip inflamed her senses, brought to life something inside her that was altogether unnerving.

'Natalie?'

The almost gentle prompting brought her back to the present and she shook herself out of her daze.

'I'm not sure that it's a good idea.'

'Neither am I, but it's the only idea I've got. Sooner or later you and I will have to meet. Your work demands it. Wouldn't it be better to meet in a civilised place and discuss the dam?'

'Oh. Is that what we're going to do?' She suddenly remembered he had said he would have dinner with her and discuss the dam and the memory rather dismayed her. She had been thinking that he just wanted to see her and her cheeks flushed as she recognised her own disappointment. She was behaving like a schoolgirl.

'What else?' he mocked, giving her the nasty feeling that he had heard the dismay in her voice.

'Well, if it's business of course I can't refuse.'

'Very gracious. I'll be there at eight. I'll book the table.' He rang off, but not before she had heard the laughter in his voice. She supposed this was all very amusing to him and when she had gone he would be right back with Annette Shelton, who looked as if she would wait for him for just about a lifetime. It must be quite dull out here for a man like Kip. Any little diversion would be welcome. Well, she was not about to be a diversion.

CHAPTER SIX

NATALIE went down to dinner in no good frame of mind, feeling a slight and hidden amount of humiliation, but, to her chagrin, Kip was right back to being the man she had first seen—cool, sardonic and just slightly disapproving. It got her more on edge than ever.

'I've ordered the team out,' she announced as they ate. 'At least, my father will now that I've told him I'm ready. They'll be here in two days.'

'And then?' He glanced up at her and she looked coolly back.

'We work and then go. Having assessed the situation I should say that two days would see us finished, three at the most—all things being equal.'

'You mean—barring accidents?'

'There will be no accidents,' Natalie said firmly, and he looked just a little scathing.

'So long as you're not breaking new ground, perhaps not.' He leaned back and looked at her levelly, his glass in his long fingers. 'You'll want to have a closer look at the dam now and get that part settled.'

'Yes, please. My father doesn't want to dwell on any drawbacks to the dam.'

'Such as?' He looked at her curiously and she faced him head on.

'The drawbacks for animals. The ecology side of things. I had plans for moving further north and seeing just what had happened when the river was diverted for a while. I also wanted to find out how many animals had been either uprooted or disturbed.'

'But your father put a stop to such plans?'

'Temporarily.'

He smiled derisively, watching the hot colour rise in her face.

'Now why should I imagine that you're saying all this to antagonise me?' he queried softly. 'Naturally, I would be all too pleased to escort you if you decide to come back—providing that I'm still here. A few more weeks and I'll have everyone trained to our methods. After that I return my house to a grateful Madembi government and I'm on my way.'

'Where?' It suddenly seemed to Natalie that the world was a very big place, dams and irrigation schemes needed all over. The chances of seeing Kip ever again were remote and, to her disquiet, the idea dismayed her.

'Who knows? India, perhaps. I know Kane has something going out there, maybe the Middle East. Like you, I never know where I'll be next, although I do stay around for longer than you appear to do.'

'Is it always you? I mean . . . what about Mr Mallory himself or some other engineer?'

'Like you, I'm the hatchet-man. Controlling the team who build a dam is not a job for a softie. Kane wants me there in future. As for going himself, I told you, he married my sister nearly four years ago. They don't like to be out of each other's sight.'

'You don't believe in that sort of love,' Natalie challenged, surprised to see a softly reminiscent look on his face.

'With Andrea and Kane, I have to believe it. The air explodes around them. For ordinary mortals, though, it's a mixture of sex and sentimentality.'

'A very comfortable thought,' Natalie pointed out tartly.

'Anything else would be very uncomfortable, pulling your life apart if you happened to be the only one who felt like that. Still, you wouldn't know anyway, would you? As I recall, you told me you'd never been in love.'

She looked away, her lips tightening. His comment about being the only one who felt like that was too close to home for her liking. Frighteningly, it didn't seem to matter any more. Neil seemed remote and she knew what she had known for days without allowing herself to face it. She could hardly remember Neil's face. When she thought of him, a coolly handsome tanned face superimposed itself over Neil's image, and mocking dark eyes seemed to haunt her dreams.

'When can I see the dam at close quarters?' she asked abruptly, firmly closing the other subject.

'Tomorrow, in the afternoon. Understand this, though, Natalie. I keep you right under my hand. I don't want you climbing on turbines. It's strictly a visit to plan the shots for your team.'

Quite clearly he had her spotted for an idiot but she needed his help so she simply nodded her agreement, praying she would get all this over with as quickly as possible before the uneasy feelings inside flowered into something utterly impossible.

She was in town the next morning when she saw Kip. He walked into the shop as she was looking for pegs, fishing about among a whole basketful for the right thing.

'Opening a laundry?' He was right behind her and the sound of his voice had her dropping her careful selection.

'They're for the shots I took. Having had films ruined in foreign parts, I develop my own. My equipment bag contains the necessary things but I've no pegs to hang them up. I'll have to set up a little darkroom in the bathroom at the hotel.'

'You enterprising creature.' He grinned down at her and turned her away, ignoring her protests. 'Luckily, I can save you a lot of trouble. The previous tenant of the government house I occupy was a photographic fanatic. He set up a small darkroom at the back of the house. You can use it.'

'Suppose I don't want to?' He already had her at the door of the shop and she set her feet firmly, looking up at him with mounting irritation. He thought he could simply arrange her life for her. Small wonder she couldn't get him out of her head.

'Then you'll be an ungrateful creature and I'll know you're scared to be with me.'

'I'm not!' Green eyes blazed at him and he smiled down at her with every appearance of satisfaction, saying not one word until she saw the humour of the situation and burst out laughing.

'You're impossible.' She laughed, allowing him to lead her to her car. 'How did you know I was in the shop anyway?'

'I saw your car in town and followed you. Now you can follow me. We'll drop in at my house so that you can inspect the set-up and Josh will give you a coffee.'

'All right.' It seemed fairly safe and in any case, she felt suddenly light-hearted, pleased to see him. The gleam in his eyes told her he knew that too.

Josh greeted her like an old friend and went off to make coffee as Kip took her to the back of the house to show her the darkroom. It looked as if at one time it might have been a room for a servant. There was water laid on and a long bench that housed all the chemicals necessary for developing photographs.

'These must be about five or six years old,' Kip warned as she inspected various bottles. 'The dishes look all right.'

'I brought my own things with me. I always do. I may as well use these dishes though. Can I do them tonight?'

She looked up eagerly and he nodded.

'Be my guest. Come for your coffee now before Josh gets annoyed.'

'What do you think that room used to be?' she asked as they moved back to the veranda, and he obviously had the same idea as she had.

'A servant's, I should think, although it's not very big. Nowadays servants have a bungalow in the grounds. Josh and Mina live at the bottom of the garden, within sight of the house.'

'You—you mean that when I was staying here I was . . . we were . . .'

'Alone? Of course.' He looked down at her with suddenly serious eyes. 'I don't remember that you suffered because of it.'

'I wasn't thinking I had. I was just realising why . . .'

'Why Annette didn't take to you on sight? I don't think it was so much her lurid imagination as her keen eyesight. You're not at all ugly. I think you were as much a shock to her as you were to me.'

'Oh, yes. I remember,' Natalie murmured, suddenly tempted to tease. 'You expected a tough female in battledress.'

'Instead I got a dream in black and gold,' he said softly. For a moment they stared at each other and when Natalie had to look away, her cheeks flushed to a soft apricot, he changed the subject smoothly.

'Quite ready for your team?'

'Yes. I wouldn't be so pleased with myself if I was still floundering.'

'I never noticed you floundering,' he confessed quietly. 'You look as if you know exactly what you're doing. It's true you get into the odd scrape, but that apart, I'm all admiration.'

'You'll see the finished film before you leave here? The minister will get a video of it. He'll be on it, speaking, of course, and so will you.'

'Me?' He looked at her suspiciously. 'Is this a trick?'

'No. You're an important part of it all. It would look astonishing if we left you out.'

For a minute she thought he was going to refuse but he watched her steadily and then nodded. 'OK. One thing at least: when you see the film in London, you'll remember me.'

Natalie looked at him for a long time, neither of them speaking. Unexpectedly she knew she would not forget Kip. It would be impossible. The knowledge showed in her green eyes for a second before she looked abruptly away.

'Neil will be interviewing you.'

'Neil?'

'He does the commentary. When they get out here I just point them in the right direction; mostly I work with Ray Hanson, the cameraman. Which reminds me,' she added, happy to have something to talk about besides remembering Kip, 'I have to hire two more vehicles. One should be a pick-up of some sort. Ray will need to ride in the back to pan the shots.'

'And where will you be?' He suddenly looked suspicious and Natalie answered without thought.

'In the back with Ray, directing him.'

'No!' She looked up, startled by his vehemence. He looked thunderous and her eyes widened at this sudden display of temper. 'If you think I'm letting you hang out of the back of a truck you're mistaken!'

'I always do.'

'Then the fact that you've not broken your beautiful neck so far is sheer good fortune. You're not doing it again.'

Natalie stood and gathered her things, looking at him with annoyance. 'Goodbye, Mr Forsythe. Thanks for the coffee.' She walked down the steps and he stood there looking after her, waiting until she got to her car before he said,

'I'll see you at the dam at two,' adding, as she nodded curtly, 'and Natalie, if you ride in the back of any truck, I give no interview.'

'The minister promised you would!' she flared at him but he simply looked mockingly sure of himself.

'I don't work for the minister. I work for Mallory-Carter. And let me tell you something, butterfly. Gabriel Basoni needs me more than he needs either you or your film. You bow to my rules or you get no interview.'

'You're impossible!' she raged, but he just nodded complacently.

'That's true.' To her vast annoyance, he simply raised his hand in farewell and went inside, leaving her to start her car and drive off angrily.

It was only as she arrived back at the hotel that two things struck her. In the first place, she would have to obey. She knew him well enough to know he didn't make idle threats. In the second place, he was worried every time she was in danger. Obviously he was a man with a highly developed sense of protectiveness. It gave her a sudden feeling of disquiet. She was capable of looking after herself. Nobody had looked after her since her mother had died. She was her father's 'right-hand man' and he never coddled her; neither had Neil. She hardly knew Kip, but he was ordering her about as if he had rights.

Natalie was a little grim-faced when she met Kip at the dam after lunch but she soon relaxed as they made a tour of the vast construction. It was almost impossible to hear each other with the steady hum of the great turbines but her camera was out and ready, the African engineers a little sheepish as they came into the shots accidentally.

Unfortunately it was necessary once again to remind Kip of the favour he had offered—the darkroom—but he simply nodded when she mentioned it.

'Come early, about five-thirty. When you've finished you can have dinner with me. I'll let Josh know.'

'Er—I have a lot of notes to write up. The team will be out tomorrow afternoon.'

She knew she was wriggling uneasily, anxious not to be alone with him, but his expression did not alter. If he knew, he was ignoring it.

'Then come at seven for dinner and do the developing later.'

There seemed to be no way out of it, and she reminded herself that Josh would be there at any rate. Only until dinner was over, though. The thought must have shown on her face.

'Afraid to be alone with me?'

'Why should I be? I've been alone with you before. I'm quite capable of taking care of myself.' It didn't seem prudent to glare at him and she managed a brief smile that met dark ironic eyes.

'I've not seen much evidence of that, but we'll let it pass for now. Dinner at seven, then. I'll get Josh to clean out the darkroom this afternoon. We wouldn't want our dainty visitor to be speckled with dust.'

She was still fuming somewhat about that when she got ready to drive to Kip's house. This obsession with her daintiness was beginning to make her feel incompetent. She had the greatest desire to wear thick trousers and boots but all that would get would be a burst of sarcasm and the inevitable laughter. In the end she wore a fairly long black skirt and a white silk blouse. If she couldn't look hefty she would look businesslike.

He didn't even seem to notice. Once again he looked elegantly casual, white, expensive jeans and a rich blue sports shirt showing off his glittering fairness, and all through the meal Natalie was subjected to a gruelling inquisition about the film. By the time the meal was over he knew as much about it as she did and she was glad to sit back with coffee and hear the end of her own voice.

'How do the rest of the team cope with your expertise—two of them being men?' he probed, just when she thought it was all over.

'Neil Bradshaw goes over the plan with me, looks at the photographs and roughly decides his commentary and the questions he'll ask people, then he takes over. I slide into the background and brief Ray Hanson.'

'What does this other girl do?'

'Paula? Just about everything else. She's Neil's handmaiden.'

It was only as she said it that Natalie realised there was a certain amount of tartness in her voice and her cheeks flushed unexpectedly.

'You dislike her?'

'On the contrary, I like her very much. Nobody could dislike Paula. She's cuddly.'

Kip's eyes narrowed, skimming over her face, an alert look about him that shook her. He missed nothing. Damn! Why did she have to answer any questions at all?

'I'll get on with the films now,' she got out hastily and Kip just nodded, leading her to the room and leaving her to it. It was a relief to close the door in the little room and be by herself. Any more questions out there and she would have been telling him about Neil.

Her preparations were almost absent-minded because her mind was dwelling on the past and her own new feelings. Now, she wasn't at all sure of what she had felt for Neil. Certainly he had not set her alight as Kip did. He was gentle and comfortable, easy to be with, and all her thwarted affection had been poured on him at a time when she was very low about the loss of her mother.

Natalie frowned as she went about her affairs slickly. Was she the sort of person who needed a man to lean on? Was that why she had felt so devastated when Neil became engaged to Paula? What was love anyway? At twenty-four she wasn't even sure, and according to Kip it was one night at a time!

The man who had set up this room had certainly been an expert, she mused as she worked. A dull red light glowed, just sufficiently bright to enable her to work, and she was glad of the quick course she had taken in developing after her precious shots had been lost in Columbia after a so-called expert's bungling.

It took longer than she had anticipated and she couldn't wait to see the final effect. She put them through the solutions and pegged them to dry, eagerly turning to switch on the lights and take a quick glimpse. A lot depended on them.

She stiffened in near horror as the lights lit up the small room. There were at least four cockroaches between her and the door, no, five—six! They had come out in the near darkness, great, long shining brutes with feelers that seemed to be searching for her.

Fright held her still, disgust shivering over her skin. It was their size that made them doubly repugnant and her lips curled in revulsion as she gathered her skirt around her. She told herself frantically that they were harmless, merely huge because of the climate, that they would be slow to move, ponderous, but as she made a slight step to the door they *did* move—like greased lightning! and everything that was feminine rose up inside her in abhorrence. She backed to the bench, screaming for Kip at the top of her voice.

He seemed to be ages coming and by the time he burst into the room her small tormenters had fled into the depths of the cupboards. She flew across to him, flinging herself into his arms, chastising him frantically and clinging to him with shaking hands.

'Why were you so long? I *needed* you!'

Belatedly she remembered and grabbed her skirt with one hand, lifting it well up as Kip held her close and looked around the room with alert but mystified eyes.

'I was outside, down by the gate. Lord, Natalie! I thought you'd been bitten by a snake!' His eyes still searched the room and then he held her away, looking into her eyes. 'What the hell is it, anyway?'

'Cockroaches!'

Her bloodcurdling whisper had his shoulders relaxing and his lips quirking in amusement.

'Oh! The heavy mob, eh?'

He was trying not to laugh but it seemed to Natalie that he wasn't trying hard enough and she pulled away stormily, clutching her skirt and glaring up at him, her hands still trembling.

'They're a sign of dirt! You should give Josh the sack!'

'They're a sign of Africa. Endemic! It's an indication of Josh's efficiency that I've seen hardly any in this house. It's just that this room is never used and the woodwork here is old. There were none here earlier.'

'It was while I had the main lights off.' She shuddered helplessly, her face filled with distaste. 'When I put the lights on they were there, six of them, blocking the way to the door!'

He looked at her outraged face and then threw his fair head back, laughing outright at her now.

'Baby, you're priceless!'

Natalie forgot her precious shots and pushed him aside, storming out on to the veranda, trembling with revulsion and rage. How typically male! How predictable! What had he expected her to do, tiptoe through them? She stiffened with annoyance as he came up to stand behind her.

'I hate you, Kip Forsythe!' She was in a rage, her dark head flung back as she stared unseeingly at the glittering stars.

'But only for a minute. I think I can stand that much.' His arms came round her waist and he pulled her back against him, holding her to the power of his body, stilling her futile struggles with strong hands.

'Let me go! I'm going to get my photographs and go back to the hotel and I'm never coming back here to this bug-infested place again. And as for you...'

His hand came to circle her throat and he tilted her head back, his eyes looking deeply into hers for a minute before his lips closed firmly over her own.

For a second she resisted him, anger still inside her, but his lips held hers drowsily, coaxing and gentle, seducing her senses, ensnaring her until she sighed against his mouth and opened her lips, inviting him to take whatever he wanted, her head pressed back against his shoulder.

His lips did not leave hers and he had no need to hold her in any sort of captivity. Her trembling now was of a different kind and she could never have moved from him. His hands ran over her arms, her shoulders with slow, languid movements until she was drained of all ability to resist. She murmured almost sleepily against his lips and his hands lifted to cup her heavy breasts and then to move inside her blouse, searching slowly for the silken curves, moving with deep, exciting rhythm until she could not stifle the sob of submission that rose in her throat.

He lifted her, curling her against him and carried her into the lamplit lounge, laying her against him on the settee, gently unfastening buttons until the creamy contours of her breasts were exposed to his gaze.

'Josh...'

'Is long gone and never comes back,' he murmured against her throat as her blouse slid from her shoulders, leaving her naked to the waist.

Natalie was so filled with exultation, so beguiled that she lay passively, a willing captive, her breasts hard and swollen beneath his searching hands, her body arching instinctively as his fair head bent and he caressed each rosy tip with gentle lips.

'My beautiful Natalie,' he whispered against her skin and even his voice seduced her, dark as black velvet, gentle, wonderful to hear.

Almost without her knowing, her own fingers reached for his shirt, her breathing slow and uneven, and the dark eyes were raised, meeting hers for a minute before he pulled the shirt over his head and lifted her towards him, bending her like a delicate flower, his hand beneath the heavy fall of her black hair, his lips claiming hers as she gasped with pleasure at the thrilling touch of his skin against hers.

She was bewitched, enslaved, caught up in an impelling fascination. No one had held her like this, looked at her, touched her, been so carefully gentle. She was floating in a new, entrancing world, lost beneath soothing hands, drowning in the sound of Kip's coaxing murmurs. As his hand reached for the zip of her skirt she moved languorously, her arms clinging to his neck, her long slender legs moving obediently as he pulled the skirt aside and tossed it to the floor.

She had no fear or thought of resistance as his hands moved possessively over her, tracing her stomach and the long slender length of her legs. She curled towards him, her green eyes wide and alluring, faintly surprised to see the taut expression on his face.

'Are you angry?'

'Angry? God!' His arms tightened at her whispered question, light flaring in his eyes as she smiled bewitchingly and entwined her arms around his neck. He stood in one swift movement, lifting her high against him, her body almost naked in his arms, and she felt no danger, no threat even when he walked into his bedroom and placed her on the bed.

Some deep, puzzled feeling was asking her why she felt no shame, why this was different. The blazing dark of Kip's eyes only excited her further and she welcomed the hard pressure of his body as it lay over her own, her whole being softening to his violent arousal.

She was so far lost that the feel of his hand sliding into the top of her lacy panties shocked her into stiffening, brought her right back to the reality of the softly lit room. Everything within her wanted to stay here but inside her head she heard his amused admission of love for one or two nights and suddenly the room stifled her, spoke to her of Annette Shelton, of other women. She stared up into his eyes, seeing the darkness narrow, probe into her mind.

'You're afraid, Natalie?'

'No. I—I . . .'

He watched her for a minute, the determined drive inside him easing, and then his hand came up to cup her flushed face as he partly assessed her problems.

'You're a virgin. Why the burning response when you're scared stiff?'

'I—I couldn't help it. You coaxed me and . . .'

'You mean I set out to seduce you?' Anger flared for a second deep in his eyes. 'Do you know how you are in my arms? Don't play such dangerous games with anyone else, butterfly, or you might not be so lucky.'

He swung off the bed and strode out of the room, coming back again before she could do more than sit up, her clothes in his hand.

'Well, you *did* warn me when we first met that you wouldn't have an affair with me,' he grated. 'Let me tell you, sweetie, that you came pretty close there.'

'I can take care of myself.' She sounded flustered, close to tears, and he took one deep controlling breath and then sat beside her, taking her blouse forcefully from her trembling fingers and dressing her whether she liked it or not.

'I've undressed you twice now,' he reminded her caustically when she protested. 'Dressing you is somewhat of a greater problem at this moment.' He slid her skirt over her head and then as her fingers searched tremblingly for the zip he suddenly ran his hand down her black shining hair. 'Calm down, Natalie. I already know you're a fake. One shrewd, businesslike television lady who turned out to be a delicate, frightened near-child.'

She opened her mouth to protest, to deny but his lips were suddenly on hers, a deep, dark pressure that warned and promised.

'Don't deny it,' he murmured against her lips, 'because if I didn't believe it you wouldn't be dressed now and ready to escape. I don't exactly enjoy being twisted up inside.'

'I—I'm sorry...'

He glanced down at her ruefully and then stood and moved to the door, leaving her to pull herself together.

'I'll collect your photographs. They should be ready by now. After that I think you'd better make your way to bed—your own this time.'

She was still trembling when she finally reached the hotel and went to bed, her body still aching with a longing she had never felt before. In the night her own voice woke her from some erotic dream and the name she was murmuring was not Neil; it was Kip, Kip, over and over again.

She was just finishing lunch the next day when Kip walked into the dining-room and sat at her table. For a minute she didn't know what to say. Feelings from last night had not left her and she was almost frantic for the others to come so that they could finish here and go home. She had just a few seconds to compose herself. Obviously he was well known here and the waiter was with them at once, bringing coffee for Kip with no other expression on his face than deference. Oddly enough that annoyed her and when he turned to her she looked at him with a carefully blank face.

As usual he defeated her, the dark, smiling eyes looking into hers.

'How are you this morning?'

'Devastated,' she wanted to say, but when the words came out they were nothing if not predictable. 'Fine! Perfectly normal.'

'I'm sorry.'

'Sorry that I'm normal?' She looked at him with as much haughtiness as she could manage but he reached across and took her hand, holding it fast when she tried to draw away.

'Sorry about last night. I took you too far, too fast. I knew damned well that you were a little innocent but I suppose I over-react to you.'

'Don't talk about me as if I'm some tender rosebud!'

She couldn't cope with this, with his gentle apology. An argument was easier to deal with and she hated the way her heart had raced when he came in. There was no future with someone like Kip and she knew it perfectly well, no future for someone like her.

'You *are* a tender rosebud, or near enough to it. I'm just finding out about you.' He sat back, letting her go. 'However, this is getting us nowhere. When does this team of yours get here?'

'Now.' As if he had conjured them up, they arrived, an airport minibus drawing up in front of the hotel.

'For three people they need a large amount of transport,' Kip murmured, standing with her and going to the foyer.

'They don't travel as light as I do,' Natalie pointed out breathlessly, so grateful for this excuse to put him at a distance. 'They have more than a tiny camera with them. This is a television unit, ready to work.'

'I'm impressed,' Kip drawled sardonically. He walked with her to the steps and then just stood there, watching, making her feel shy and nervous as she faced her own people at last after what seemed like a lifetime of parting.

It stunned her to realise that they didn't seem quite real. Suddenly only Kip was real and she was definitely over-enthusiastic as Ray greeted her with fierce hugs and his usual extravagant words.

'Natalie! The love of my life!'

He lifted her off her feet and swung her round and she laughed into his face but all the time she was aware of Kip's mocking expression and she dreaded facing Neil.

For a minute, Neil didn't look at her. He was turning to help Paula out and then giving instructions about the equipment.

'Natalie! What a fabulous place!' Paula was quite normal; soft, bubbly and completely open. 'Gosh! What are those birds?' Natalie was explaining about the crested cranes when Neil finally turned. None of them seemed to realise that the tall, fair man watching was anything to do with them at all, but to Natalie his stillness and slightly ironic interest was overpowering. He was summing them up, and it never took Kip long to do that.

She was in a state of agitation, wondering what he would think, unable to sort her own mind out because the touch of his hand on hers was still with her, more real than the extravagant hugs that Ray had bestowed on her.

Paula and Ray walked to the edge of the huge lawns, looking out over the dam, obviously a little overawed in spite of their experience, and it was then that Neil turned and looked at her.

'Natalie?'

She smiled at him, wanting to keep her distance, but he walked over, his glance sweeping over her almost greedily, his hand tilting her chin when he got close.

'Been a good girl?' He was standing too close, his eyes on her lips, and she stepped back quickly, uncomfortably aware of Kip's gaze and of Paula so close by.

'What an odd thing to ask me. I've been working like mad.'

'You've been ill.'

'Only a little virus, I assure you,' she informed him lightly, desperate to move off. What was the matter with him? He was behaving almost possessively.

'So far away from home. I should have been here with you.'

'I can't think of one good reason why.' Her eyes turned warningly to Paula, who was just coming back, and Neil stepped away, pivoting to meet the blue-eyed blonde who wore his ring.

'Well, what do you think of it?' There was the same possession, indulgence in his voice that he had used to Natalie, although this time there was not the intent expression. His arm went round Paula's shoulders as he drew her close and Natalie felt a wave of unaccustomed fury at him. What was he playing at? Paula might be a cuddly little blonde but she certainly wasn't blind, nor was she stupid.

CHAPTER SEVEN

NATALIE swung round to introduce them to Kip and found his face set in harsh lines of disapproval. Of course, he never missed anything, and he would have had to be blind to miss that!

'This is Kip Forsythe, who is in charge of the dam,' she said more firmly than she felt. It was impossible to meet those dark, scathing eyes. He made her feel guilty, as if *she* was the one at fault. Even so, she introduced them all carefully and Kip was, as ever, completely polite, with a very special smile for Paula which apparently didn't much endear him to Neil.

'We'll get up to our rooms and then perhaps you could brief me, Natalie?' Neil turned away after the terse sentence and Natalie wasn't about to let him get away with it. She felt harassed from all sides and came out fighting.

'I'll brief you *all*!' He had really rattled her and she was embarrassed and unnerved by Kip's steady gaze. 'There's a very nice lounge here that will just do.' If he thought she was about to go to his room he could think again. She was astonished at her change of heart, but in any case she never had been able to stand treachery and it seemed to her that Paula was heading for heartbreak.

'Really? I thought *I* was in charge.' Her tone of voice and obvious manoeuvre had not escaped Neil and he turned on her with narrowed eyes.

'Mention it to Father!'

Ray and Paula looked astonished but they said nothing, all following an obviously angry Nell into the hotel. Natalie fought to gain control of her temper and Kip walked slowly down the steps to tower over her, making her feel small and altogether negligible.

'If that was for my benefit then you didn't really need to bother,' he informed her coldly.

'I don't exactly know what you mean.' Natalie looked up at him with a great deal of challenge in her green eyes although she almost cringed at the scorn.

'You do. We speak the same language, you and I, amazing though it may seem to you, and I don't need a written explanation to sum up a situation. I now understand your supreme touchiness too. Was he your lover before or after the little blonde?'

Her hand flashed up to strike him, almost without thought, but he was too fast for her, grasping her wrist and holding on. An undignified struggle was not possible right here at the front of the hotel, although it didn't seem to bother Kip. All she could do was glare at him and she did.

'There are no lovers in my life. I thought you'd fathomed that. How disappointing. I imagined you knew everything.'

Her long green eyes blazed up at him. At that moment she hated all men—Kip too. He said nothing at all, still holding on to her wrist, probing her mind with dark eyes, searching for the truth until she began to drown in the darkness, the hot, bright sunlight forgotten.

'There's trouble coming from that direction,' he informed her curtly after she felt the world begin to give way beneath her feet. 'The little blonde is about to be hurt. I see she wears a ring. His?'

'They're engaged and her name is Paula. Neil was perhaps a little extravagant in greeting me but I've known him a long time. Come to think of it, I'd better go and make my peace with him. I've never pulled the Daddy's girl bit before. He annoyed me.'

'He embarrassed you because I was there,' Kip corrected, looking down at her. Tall, lean and fit, sure of himself as ever, he unnerved her tremendously. 'No man behaves like that without encouragement.'

'You went a good deal further than that...' Natalie began and then stopped in horror, her face flooding with colour.

'There is a difference,' he pointed out scathingly. 'I'm quite free to want you. Bradshaw is engaged.' He let her go and turned away, dismissing her so completely that she cringed. 'Let me know your timetable,' he added coolly. 'I'll be available.'

'Well, I *won't* be!' There were tears in her eyes and she couldn't work out why. It hurt to have Kip think badly of her. Why was she getting herself into this?

'I'm thinking about the necessity to work with your team, to face the all-seeing eye of the camera.' He turned at his car to hand out this final slap and Natalie swirled away, her skirts flying, heading into the hotel and her own room, humiliation making her tremble all over.

'I think we should invite him to dinner.' Neil dropped his bombshell quietly into the silence at the end of the briefing and Natalie stiffened, near-panic spreading over her.

'I'm sure he won't be free at such short notice. He's a very busy man.'

'Not too busy to be here when we arrived,' Neil pointed out tightly.

'We had things to discuss.' She wondered why she was explaining things to Neil and also why he was so bent on forcing the subject. His easygoing attitude seemed to have deserted him.

'Didn't you stay with him while you were ill?' Ray asked, and she detected a note of goading in his voice that was certainly not aimed at her.

Undercurrents seemed to be swirling around her, things she had never noticed before, Ray's eyes watching for Neil's reaction to this information.

'He was very kind to me. I wasn't really fit to be in a hotel. His servant's wife nursed me, actually. I don't really know what I would have done without Kip.'

'Forsythe seems to be a big wheel in these parts.' Ray was clearly driving home some point of his own and Natalie firmly squashed it while she still could.

'His firm built the dam and the owner of the firm is his brother-in-law. Kip is also a great friend of the minister's. It's as well to keep on the right side of him, actually, especially as we'll need his help while we're here. Believe me, if he pulls out, we're stuck.'

She went off to discuss the photographs with Ray while Paula and Neil strolled in the grounds and as soon as they were on their own she tackled him.

'How do you know I stayed with Kip Forsythe while I was ill?'

'Your old man told me—inadvertently, I'll admit.' He wasn't grinning in his usual manner and Natalie looked at him in exasperation.

'What's wrong with you, anyway?'

'Neil Bradshaw's wrong with me. I could smash his smug face in—maybe I will.' He turned to walk over to the window, hands in his pockets, frustration in every line of his body, and Natalie watched, almost open-mouthed.

'You ... ?'

'The most mild-mannered of men,' he finished for her in a rasping voice. 'I'm sick of him in more ways than one. Sick of him throwing his weight about for one thing.'

'He's good at his job——' Natalie began but he cut her off ruthlessly.

'Aren't we all? Isn't that what this unit is about, small and excellent? I can tell you I was delighted to hear you put him down when we came.'

'Well, I'm ashamed of it.' She was, thinking about the reason why she had acted so out of character. 'He was quite a big producer before he joined us. In fact I can't think why he *did* join us.'

'Come off it, kiddo! He took one look at you!'

'And then he took one look at Paula,' Natalie snapped. 'What's this all about? You've never listened to anyone in your life, so why is Neil getting under your skin?'

'Paula,' Ray said tautly. 'She's heading for a big hurt. She's so innocent, poor little thing. It's all Bradshaw can do to keep his hands off you.'

'Well, he's managed so far,' Natalie snapped, 'and I think you're exaggerating.'

It was only last night that Kip had thought *she* was an innocent creature. Now he thought she was some sort of a *femme fatale*. He had come to make it up with her at lunchtime, she was sure of it, and now she was right back to square one. She wished the team had not come out. She wished she were back in London. Much more of this and she would scream at everybody.

When she went back out Neil was looking very pleased with himself. She even noticed the smugness for the first time ever.

'I got Forsythe's number from Reception, Natalie,' he announced with a clever look that had her fuming. 'He'll be delighted to come. I told him to bring his girlfriend. That makes three men and three women. A nice little dinner party.'

'We're not here to give dinner parties!' Natalie blazed, but he simply smiled and dropped his tone to tenderness.

'It's going to be dark in an hour. It's too late to do anything else, love.' Love! She saw Paula's eyes widen and Ray's darken with annoyance but neither of them knew how *she* felt. Kip would bring Annette Shelton and she would have to watch them together. It mattered to her now, she admitted it.

'Damn!' She glared at Neil and then stormed off to her room, leaving them to think what they liked. One more minute there and she would have burst into tears of frustration. Much longer in Africa and she wouldn't have either a mind or a heart of her own. She hated all men, Ray, Neil and even Kip.

The only two people here who were blameless were Paula and herself and they were the ones who were going to be hurt because she knew right now that Neil would never stick to his fiancée. She also knew that it would hurt badly to see Kip with Annette tonight, especially as she knew what would happen when they left the hotel after dinner.

He brought Annette, not that Natalie had expected anything else. It was almost a gesture of defiance in her that made her wear the black and gold she had worn when she had first seen him. She had thought a long time about what to wear and the sight of the outfit she had arrived in had clinched it, some perverse longing to go back in time. It was only when Kip's eyes narrowed over her that she remembered this was the outfit she had been wearing when she had first gone to his house, when he had undressed her and put her to bed, the first time she had felt his hands on her skin.

'You look beautiful,' Neil murmured in her ear, and she felt herself stiffen with the flare of impending trouble that now seemed to hang around her almost permanently.

Ray also noticed the small, familiar gesture and annoyance rose at once. He moved protectively towards Paula and Natalie felt swamped by events that had caught up with her without any move on her part to precipitate them. She felt like someone plunging headlong into a crisis, and her normal character surfaced. She would have liked to be cool, aloof, but this was a dinner for an important man, a man who watched everything and everybody with keen all-seeing eyes.

She glittered, a flow of nervous energy making her brilliantly beautiful. She seemed to be talking endlessly, keeping everyone laughing, her long green eyes flashing with enthusiasm that nobody could see was forced. Always slender, she had lost weight in Africa and as the evening wore on it seemed that she would either have to stop, slow down or break into pieces.

She was holding the attention of all the men without even trying, everything as she had not in any way intended, and Annette's eyes took on a tendency to turn to ice as each movement in the conversation seemed to bring things back to Natalie.

Kip brought things to a sudden halt.

'How would you all like to end the evening at the club?' he suddenly asked.

'There's a club here?' Neil looked just a little scathing. He had drunk too much and was almost on a high to match Natalie's although she had drunk hardly anything at all.

'Wherever Europeans are, they set up a club,' Kip informed him drily. 'Ours is for swimming, golf and a variety of social activities. Tonight there's a dance.'

'Oh, dear! You mean we dragged you away from it? You would have been there now if you hadn't been attending this business dinner?' Natalie asked, smiling brilliantly, her voice almost brittle with exhaustion.

'Probably.' Kip looked at her with a great deal of irony. 'We don't seem to have discussed much business, but it's been very entertaining.'

'Natalie's a jewel,' Neil declared, leaning back complacently, his remarks bringing puzzled anxiety to Paula's face, a flush of embarrassment to Natalie's.

'If we're going, I'll freshen up,' Natalie said quickly, animation dying from her face.

The men stood and so did Paula, moving with Natalie to the powder-room with an air of desperation about her that made Natalie wince. She didn't have to wait long.

'Natalie?' There were tears in her eyes as she spoke and Natalie's heart sank like a stone. It was no use pretending she didn't understand.

'Drink talks loudly,' she said soothingly, trying her best to smile. 'I don't think Neil's quite used to it.'

'He wasn't drunk earlier. I know he used to go out with you. He's still in love with you, isn't he?'

'He's not and he never was.' Natalie turned to Paula firmly. 'At the moment he's being childish for some reason I can't fathom. But you can forget about anything between Neil and me. There never was anything and there never will be. I admire his work, nothing more.'

'Then you're not in love with him?' Paula's eyes met Natalie's in the mirror as Natalie combed her long, black hair, and she didn't pause for thought.

'I'm not and I never was.' How clear it seemed now. Neil meant nothing to her at all except that at the moment he was a distinct source of irritation. She had never loved him; how could she have thought it? All she could see was Kip—Kip with the burning dark eyes. Kip with his power and grace. The comb almost fell from her hand. She loved him, that was why she flared with heat each time he touched her. He did well to call her a child. The knowledge stunned her.

'Natalie? Are you all right?' Paula touched her arm and Natalie snapped back to the present.

'Fine, just fine.'

'I didn't upset you—about Neil, I mean?'

'Of course not. He's your problem and I for one would give him a hefty kick. He's about due for it.'

They were both giggling as they made their way to the foyer where the others were waiting, and it seemed to Natalie that all the men were looking at them a trifle anxiously, Kip of course with more derision than anxiety. Maybe they had expected a fight in the powder-room? Paula walked determinedly to Neil, taking his arm in what looked like a judo grip, and Natalie burst into laughter, whirling towards the door, her skirt flying around her, the yellow flowers bright cascades of colour against the black.

'Let's go!' she sang out brightly.

Kip was beside her in two strides, taking her arm and pulling her close to his side, his voice low and commanding.

'Slacken off,' he ordered abruptly. 'Go on like this and you'll shatter into bits.'

Her heart started fluttering as soon as his fingers touched her skin and he felt the tremors of feeling rush through her.

'I'm enjoying myself!' She carefully did not look at him, afraid now to give herself away, her knowledge too new to be faced.

'The hell you are! You're just about ready to spin off the world, and all with three sips of wine. You should be either spanked soundly or put to bed—probably both.'

'I'm not tired!' She looked up at him defiantly, her blue-black hair emphasising her olive skin, her softly tinted cheeks, her eyes blazing green, more alluring than she would ever know.

'Did I mention sleep?' His eyes burned into hers. 'Be thankful for vast crowds, beautiful. I could eat you with no difficulty at all.' She shuddered with feeling and his hand tightened, sheer male satisfaction in his eyes. 'You're surely asking for it,' he growled. 'Now, behave yourself. Our club is respectable, all passions carefully hidden.'

'Oh? How does Annette manage, then?' She had a desire to drive him to some form of retaliation, to goad him into action, her feelings bubbling up inside, ready to overwhelm her.

'Annette? She's a calm headmistress, butterfly.'

The calm headmistress arrived beside them, almost breathless, grasping Kip's arm like a vice.

'Darling! I hope you haven't been telling her off? She's really entertaining when she lets herself go.' Her blue eyes were everywhere, questioning, probing, inspecting Natalie's flushed face and Kip's sardonic satisfaction.

'But she never lets herself go, do you, Natalie?' he murmured sardonically. 'We have here a television lady in action, entertaining contacts.'

'So long as there's not too much contact, darling.' Annette chortled; at least she meant to chortle but it came out so shrilly that the others, coming up looked with an equal amount of suspicion at both Natalie and Kip.

'My partner, I think,' Ray said firmly, taking Natalie's arm and marching her off to the cars. 'What did you say to Paula?' he enquired softly. 'She seems to have improved. She might even take a swing at Bradshaw herself and save me the trouble.'

'Dear me,' Natalie sighed mockingly. 'Everybody wants a quiet word with me.'

'I'll not ask about Forsythe's words if you tell me about Paula,' Ray said artfully. 'It's obvious what he would like to say to you. Watch out for that Annette person. She looks the sort of woman to have a dagger in her stocking-top.'

'You're fairly crude,' Natalie informed him, giggling with an unaccustomed feeling of light-headedness.

'I manage.' He grinned down at her. 'Let's get back to Paula and the discussion.'

'Are you my friend, Ray?' she suddenly asked seriously, the excitement and burning feelings leaving her all at once, making her feel just too vulnerable.

'Well, I always have been. I'm a safe friend, dear thing, because, for reasons I can never fathom, I'm not in love with you.'

'Thank you, Ray,' she said as solemnly as a child. 'I may need a friend.'

'Look no further. Can you manage to calm down, do you think? Forsythe looks as if he's considering violence, then there's the Annette with her own brand. Let's talk like two old buddies.'

'I expect you're in love with Paula?' Natalie mused as he handed her into her own car and proceeded to take the wheel without so much as a by-your-leave, a fact that greatly reassured her. Asked to drive, she would probably have ended up with everyone in the dam.

'With Paula? Yes. That's just about it.' He sounded very grim and Natalie touched his arm consolingly.

'I'm really sorry, Ray.'

'Not to worry, love. Just so long as she's happy.'

'Who's happy?' Natalie murmured quietly, and he gave a short bark of laughter.

'Not a damned one of us on this expedition as far as I can see.'

Neil and Paula came to join them, both sliding into the back of the car as Ray waited for Kip to lead the way in his own vehicle.

'What was Forsythe saying to you?' Neil asked before they had even got started and Natalie felt like turning and beating him up.

'For God's sake!' Ray muttered under his breath but Paula nearly took their breath away, the bit between her teeth.

'I don't think anyone should ask her that,' she said firmly, quite outside her normal childlike character. 'Kip Forsythe is wildly in love with Natalie; it's as plain as the nose on your face.'

'Whose face?' Neil scoffed with just a touch of sharpness in his voice. 'Honestly, my pretty, you say such ridiculous things.'

'You'll see,' Paula snapped, suddenly annoyed at the patronising tone. 'His eyes eat her up and no wonder; she's beautiful.'

'That hasn't escaped my notice—ever,' Neil answered with an almost deliberate cruelty that infuriated Natalie.

With any girl less gentle than Paula he would have been tipped out of the car then and left to walk. 'Does he eat you up, Natalie, love?' He sounded so damned sure of his own charms that Natalie couldn't let it pass; besides, she was behind Paula one hundred per cent.

'Well, he hasn't yet, but we've considered it,' she murmured coyly. 'It's all very private, if you don't mind.'

Ray shot her a look of astonishment and then grinned in the darkness as he saw the angry glitter of her eyes, her lovely mouth set tightly. Paula sat back, vindicated, a small smile of satisfaction on her face. This trip to Africa was making her see Neil in an entirely new light. He needed a strong hand and her own little hands were not so fluttery as he imagined. There was a great deal of strength in a determined woman, however young.

Neil said nothing. In the darkness of the car his scowl was as black as the night. Natalie was *his*, whenever he wanted her! He must have been mad to let her go. Had all that glitter, all that passionate, nervy excitement tonight been for Forsythe? It seemed to him that Annette Shelton was more than a dear friend, more likely a frequent visitor to Forsythe's bed. Natalie didn't stand a chance. He grunted in satisfaction, his mind cleared of doubt, and then said nothing at all.

The club was a low, modern building arranged around three sides of a large swimming-pool. It had taken a drive across town to get there and there was sufficient light coming from the windows and balconies for Natalie to see that a golf course spread around it, reaching across to the river.

That there was a dance in progress was obvious; music came drifting across to the car park and the festive feeling hit them as soon as they stepped inside.

'Oh, I say! It's lovely!' Paula's enthusiasm brought a grin to Kip's face and he glanced down at her approvingly.

'No shortage of tropical blooms to adorn the place,' he pointed out, nodding to the great displays of flowers that decorated the rooms.

'Oh, I thought you meant the ladies!' Paula surprised herself and everyone else and Kip looked as if he was about to pat her on the head like a good girl. She had plenty of spirit now, not at all as she had been when she went to the powder-room with Natalie.

His eyes flashed to Natalie's face, seeing her look of satisfaction at this turn of events, and his expression softened, the smile back in his eyes as their glances clashed. So she was a good girl and the boss approved. She turned away fretfully and was grateful to Ray when he scooped her away to the floor, dancing her out of reach of trouble.

'Dearest friend to the rescue,' he muttered. 'Watch your step, *Natalia mio*. Annette Thingummy is gunning for you.'

'I don't damned well care,' Natalie snapped. 'I could boil everybody in a vat of hot oil!'

Ray laughed and put his cheek against her hair, swirling her round to the music, singing, 'Love is the Sweetest Thing' under his breath, at total variance with the music.

'I'll crown you,' Natalie muttered, not at all amused, too tight inside to see anything funny at all.

'All right. All right.' He patted her shoulder and slowed down. 'Thanks, love. Somehow or other you've opened Paula's eyes. Maybe it will do me no good but I'm damned glad anyway. She might just surprise

Bradshaw. At any rate, *you've* given him an obvious snub.'

'By lying in my teeth,' Natalie pointed out, a bit anxious about her earlier boldness.

'I wonder?' Ray looked down at her suspiciously, and she gave him a small grimace of disgust.

'Please, Ray. Don't trouble your pretty head about me.'

They were both laughing as they left the floor and Neil was dancing with Paula, looking as if he had little alternative.

'Drink, Natalie?' Kip looked across at her, his eyes brilliantly alive, and she could only nod, her feelings suddenly too much for her. If he had ordered her to move towards him she would have done. Her gaze was fixed on his face, all the life in her drained into her radiant eyes.

'I think I'll keep you on white wine,' he said softly. 'Any mixing of drinks and you'll probably take off into the stratosphere.'

'Perhaps she's drunk too much already?' Annette snapped. 'She looks pretty odd to me.'

'She never drinks!' Ray came immediately to her rescue but Kip did not take his eyes off Natalie's face. There was a look about her he couldn't mistake and he wanted to get her out of here, cursing himself for offering this outing. She looked quite incapable of defending herself.

'She's had about four sips of wine all evening,' he pointed out calmly. 'Another sip or two won't hurt her.'

'I'll help to carry the drinks,' Ray offered, quite approving of Kip Forsythe, and Natalie was left alone, a bristling opponent close beside her.

'Keep your delicate little claws off Kip!' Annette hissed as soon as the men were out of sight. 'He's mine and that's exactly how things are going to stay.'

'I beg your pardon?' Natalie stood quite shocked at the openly vicious attack, staring into the pale blue eyes that glared at her. It was a funny thing about blue, she thought dazedly. Paula had lovely blue eyes. These eyes were glittering with an almost feral rage.

'You heard me and you understand. Don't think I haven't noticed your little tricks. You've got the other two men hanging around your neck; leave Kip alone.'

'Suppose he won't allow that?' Natalie was stung to reply.

'How long are you here for? Two more days, three? I've had him for a lot longer than that and I'm keeping him. I'm not wasting my time. I've no intention of spending my life with a pack of simpering schoolkids. Kip's brother-in-law is a millionaire and Kip's part of it. His baby sister dotes on him and Kane Mallory dotes on her.'

'I see. You want a meal ticket,' Natalie said flatly, her eyes scornful.

'Oh, not only that. Kip is a very satisfying man, if you understand me.'

'I understand you,' Natalie said in disgust, the dazzling light dying in her green eyes.

When Kip came back, she took her drink with a muttered thanks and turned away, not looking at him. Annette hung on to his arm with every intention of staying there and Ray as ever became Natalie's protector.

'Well, I'll say this for you,' he murmured as they took their drinks and walked to the area around the brilliantly lit pool, 'you surely need a friend. What did she say to you during our brief absence? Not got a knife sticking in you anywhere, have you?'

'She's not important,' Natalie managed a little desperately. After all, she hadn't learned anything she wasn't already well aware of, except perhaps Annette's greed. The thought of Kip's arms around anyone else was just about killing her; no knife could have done any better.

'She feels important, I would say,' Ray surmised. 'She's hooked on to Forsythe's arm like an umbrella.'

'Bless you, Ray.' She smiled up at him. 'I'm glad to see this particular part of the team at any rate.'

'You'll keep on protecting me from your dad?'

'Ferociously.'

He draped his arm around her shoulders and they walked slowly around the pool.

'Two miserable wretches, you and I. Both very sadly in love.'

'*I'm* not in love!' Natalie protested, but he gave her a glance that was both scathing and rueful.

'Kiddo, when he looks at you, you glow. If that's not love, then you're very ill indeed.'

'I'd rather be ill any day,' Natalie said fervently, stiffening as Kip strolled out to meet them, Annette still clutching him fiercely.

His eyes settled on Natalie with such determination that she felt a quiver run over her skin.

'As host to this part of the evening, I'm claiming a dance,' he said firmly. She wanted to refuse but his gaze was fixed on her inflexibly and she just seemed to float forward, straight into the arms that lifted to receive her.

'Hold my drink, Ray?' Kip handed his drink across, his other arm securing Natalie to his side, and Ray beamed at him, immensely pleased to be called by his first name. He had heard Kip Forsythe say 'Bradshaw' with a great deal of distaste. Another one up on the odious Neil, he thought grimly. Not that he wanted to be left with the Annette woman; she looked mad enough to hold him under the water.

Her eyes followed Kip and Natalie—he could almost see her thinking and seething. Those two looked so right together, almost a part of each other. Natalie was tucked under Kip's shoulder like a delicate piece of china except that she was yielding and soft. If he could see it, then this madwoman couldn't miss it.

Natalie felt anything but yielding. She held herself stiffly away as Kip drew her to the dance-floor.

'I'm really not happy to leave Ray with Annette,' she snapped, controlling her trembling by sheer force of will. 'She looks all succulent and tropical, like a Venus fly trap.'

'Don't be spiteful. It doesn't suit you,' Kip said in a hard voice. 'And you can relax.'

'Thank you. I prefer not to.'

He pulled her tightly against him, almost angrily. 'It wasn't a suggestion. It was an order.'

'Well, you can't order *me* about!' It was terrible the way it was hurting to think of his arms around Annette, and more besides. She suddenly found tears blinding her eyes and he knew without even looking at her.

'What did Annette say to you?' he asked softly, his hold slackening to gentleness.

'Nothing I didn't already know. She just painted the picture more brightly. Very descriptive.'

'And of course you believed her.'

'I know about your love-affairs, Mr Forsythe. You enlightened me yourself, if you recall.'

'Never with Annette,' he said harshly.

'You expect me to believe that?'

'Not particularly. It's just that I like the sound of the truth for my own sake. Annette makes her feelings quite plain. Unfortunately, I can't go along with her, ungallant though it may seem.'

'I don't know why you're telling me this saga. I have nothing to do with it at all. I couldn't care less.'

He tilted her chin firmly, forcing her to look at him.

'Try lying to my face, Natalie,' he suggested quietly. His expression softened as he saw the tears. 'You certainly know how to get to me, don't you? All I want to do right now is pick you up and carry you off.'

'You'll just have to stop treating me like a child,' Natalie told him, her voice trembling.

'Just give me the chance.' His dark voice shivered across her skin, catching every quivering nerve-end, and she was utterly lost, not one defence in sight.

'All right.' He relented and turned back to the area of the pool where now quite a few people had gathered, laughing, talking, some of them balancing plates of food from the buffet. 'I'll let you off the hook for now, but don't think it's going to go away.'

'That's all right. *I'm* going to go away.'

'And maybe I'll be right behind you,' he promised softly.

And maybe he wouldn't. Wanting wasn't loving, and she had found out far too late how she could feel. She had been too inexperienced to recognise any of the signs, although now they were glaringly obvious.

CHAPTER EIGHT

NEIL was by the pool with Paula and Ray, the latter still cradling Kip's drink and his own. Of Annette there was no sign and that was a relief until Natalie saw Neil's thunderous looks. Everywhere she turned there seemed to be problems. She greeted Ray almost hysterically.

'Enjoying yourself?' Neil looked about as happy as a sick crocodile, Paula standing somewhat subdued beside him. Evidently her new-found strategies had waned and Natalie felt too upset to help right now.

She ignored Neil completely, tucking her arm in Ray's and hoping that Kip would just go. This evening couldn't end soon enough for her. She wished she had pleaded a headache and stayed at the hotel.

'We'll have a little dance,' Ray suggested, sweeping her up and getting into the beat of the music. He looked a bit frantic; maybe soon he would have everyone on his hands, Paula as well as Natalie. Just so long as he didn't get Annette he would cope, but he was worried by Natalie's sudden pallor. Somebody should lock Annette up.

The other couples there took up the idea and soon a small crowd were circling the pool, laughing and screeching as they sometimes came dangerously close to the edge. Natalie couldn't get into any party spirit now. She had exhausted herself much earlier and she slid out of Ray's arms.

'Sorry, partner. I've had enough. I'll sit out if you don't mind.'

135

One minute she was looking into his rueful eyes and the next she was almost sailing through the air, straight into the water that looked pale green and cold and felt very cold indeed as it closed over her head. Somebody had pushed her, somebody who almost caught Ray too. She had a vague feeling of seeing him tottering and then righting his balance, consternation on his face as he shouted her name hoarsely.

She surfaced, barely seeing the ring of faces that surrounded the pool, all looking at her as if she were stark raving mad. She struck out for the side and saw Kip push Ray away and reach for her himself, lifting her out and holding her steady.

Water was pouring from her, from her dress and her long black hair and she looked into Kip's angry face like a lost soul.

'My sandal came off.' Oddly enough, it was all she could think to say. His lips tightened to one straight line, more angry still by the look of him.

'I'll get someone to fish it out. Right now you've got to get dry.'

Annette seemed to pop up like an evil Jack-in-the-box. 'What an odd thing to do. I knew she'd had too much to drink. How embarrassing.'

'Oh, she does plenty of odd things,' Kip said with an air of someone who knew her every move.

'I'll take her back,' Ray said furiously, glaring at Annette, but Kip shook his head grimly.

'My duty, I believe. Perhaps you could drop Annette off on your way back, Ray?'

'A pleasure,' Ray said bravely, adding in a low voice, 'right over the dam.' He knew perfectly well who had pushed Natalie. He had seen those hideously blue eyes right behind her just as she was about to walk off. There was no way he could prove it and he took a great deal of satisfaction in watching Annette's angry face as Kip took Natalie firmly in hand and got her out of the club.

In the car Kip said nothing at all and it upset her terribly. Another time when he had been obliged to rescue her. It was written right across his face.

'Ray could have brought me. There was no need to leave Annette,' she said miserably, and he rounded on her with flashing eyes as if he was about to beat her.

'Shut up!' His voice was quiet savagery. 'I know damned well how you came to be in that pool.'

'I'm a disaster area,' she murmured. 'A problem waiting to happen.'

'Not with somebody's hand in the small of your back, giving a hefty push,' he gritted.

'You saw it?'

'My God, no! There's nothing wrong with my mental computer, though.' He turned on the heating. 'I'll have you back at the hotel as quickly as possible. You'd be more comfortable with me but I know better than to suggest it.'

She didn't answer that because suddenly she wanted to be with Kip, on any terms.

'I never got my sandal.'

'I'll get it to you tomorrow,' he snapped. 'It's not important.'

'They're Italian. Fifty-nine pounds.'

He shot her a look of astonishment and then drove grimly on, scowling at passing cars. 'One day you'll drive me completely insane,' he growled. 'Sometimes I could choke you.'

'Because I worry about wasting so much money? Italian shoes are expensive.'

'Be quiet, Natalie, or I'll shake the life out of you,' he threatened, and she knew when to stop. In this mood he might just do it and a shaking was more than she could handle right now.

At the hotel he took her right to her room, robbing the incident of her appearance of all embarrassment, explaining to several members of the hotel staff that she had been in an accident. Of course he carried it off with his usual self-assurance and as they arrived at her door there was a maid on hand offering to wash her 'beautiful clothes' at once.

'Right. That lets me out,' Kip said grimly as she stood rather pitifully out in the corridor. 'Get to bed, Natalie. This hasn't been your day.'

'Tomorrow I'll be right as rain,' she assured him defiantly. She wanted to cling to him but nothing in the world would have made her do it.

'We'll see,' he muttered. He turned and walked away, tall and aloof, and she went quickly into her room before she surrendered to the urge to race after him or beg him to stay.

In the morning it was all too clear that Neil had a bad head. He was all ill-tempered producer, a white sun-hat pulled almost over his eyes and dark sunglasses on his nose.

'Let's move!' he ordered as they finished breakfast.

Throughout the meal there had been none of the normal joking and chatter that was part of their working relationship. Paula was looking pale and miserable and Ray was still darkly brooding. As to Neil's bad head, it served him right. If he hadn't thought up the small dinner party none of the previous night's events would have happened.

It looked too as if he was about to 'come the heavy'—as Ray put it, something that none of them did. Apparently he imagined he was back in his old job and meant to behave like a producer in a studio. It promised trouble because neither Natalie nor Ray would swallow that. Their set-up was totally different and they all knew it.

Neil looked askance at the vehicle Natalie had managed to get. Her original idea of a pick-up had met with such opposition from Kip that she had abandoned that idea. It was no use defying him. If she was working in the back of a pick-up he would refuse an interview and she knew it perfectly well. She had hired an open Land Rover, uncomfortable but practical. It would do for all of them and the camera could be propped against the back hoops, so could the sound boom. At least she would *look* safer there.

'I thought you were getting two cars?' Neil liked comfort, she knew, but this morning she was not in any sort of pliant mood. She had spent a miserable night thinking about Kip and she wanted the team away before he decided to investigate their affairs.

'Things aren't all that easy to come by here,' she muttered, helping Ray to set up the telescopic boom for the sound. 'This will do. We're not going to be in it long.'

'Only for the whole damned day!' Neil snapped, wincing at the pain that shot through his head at this display of temper.

'Shall I do the sound?' Paula enquired in a miserable voice.

'Yes. Natalie can sit by me and help.'

'Help with what?' Natalie asked shortly. 'I'll do the sound. In any case, Ray's going to need me in all probability.'

'Who's supposed to be in charge of this expedition?'

Neil took his sunglasses off to glare at her and Natalie spun round on him, handing out glare for glare.

'It looks as if I am. It's going to take you all your time to keep upright by the look of you!'

None of them had noticed Kip's car coming up the long drive of the hotel. He was leaning against it, watching this interesting scene, but then so were half the staff of the hotel and Natalie was beyond caring, her temper flaring.

Evidently her annoyance had managed to penetrate Neil's arrogance and his befuddled brain. He grimaced and tried a sickly smile.

'God knows why I drank so much last night,' he offered in a placating tone.

'Sheer stupidity?'

Natalie swung herself up into the back of the Land Rover, scorning help. Temper had given her a certain amount of athletic agility and her slender body, in jeans and vividly red T-shirt, was vibrantly alive, quivering with annoyance. This morning she had tied her long hair back, ready for action and looking it.

'Hand it up.' She was even snapping at Ray, but she got an impudent grin as he passed the assembled boom to her and she strapped it securely to the hoops, testing its ability to swing and reaching for the huge microphone that would pick up the sound of water, the thunder of the dam and hopefully the terrifying sound of the Tamberi Falls.

She was kneeling in the back, checking the sound equipment, when Kip strolled over and looked down at her.

'Hello, beautiful. You're on the rampage this morning?'

She looked up quickly at the sound of his voice and then looked away again with even greater speed. The way the sunlight caught his fair hair made her heart turn over and she wanted to scream at him for everything, for making her love him, for Annette, for being here at all.

'I'm surrounded by idiots!' she snapped.

'I'll have your apology in writing,' Ray murmured, springing up beside her.

'Oh, I don't mean you or Paula,' she muttered, afraid to look up and meet Kip's dark eyes.

'Then it must be Bradshaw and me,' Kip surmised.

'*You* said it!'

He showed his superb strength by reaching in and lifting her bodily out to stand in front of him, his hands still tightened round her tiny waist.

'Where are you going today?' he asked with such quiet authority that she did not think of telling him to mind his own business.

'Everywhere. Tomorrow there's the opening ceremony so everything else has to be done today. We'll just have time to do the aerial shots in the morning.'

'Aerial shots? How are you going to manage that?'

'The minister offered a plane when I went down to see him.'

'And of course you never considered telling me?' His hands tightened, making her feel breathless.

'I—I forgot.' Why didn't she tell him to keep out of her affairs? The truth was she dared not. He looked grim and angry suddenly. A few seconds before there had been a lazy indulgence in his voice; now there was cold steel.

'She's not going up,' Ray said hastily, mistaking the sudden heightening of tension. 'It's something I do alone.'

'Make sure she doesn't sneak on board.' Kip let her go and turned away and Neil, coming back, just had time to grab his attention before he stalked off.

'I'd like to do the interview with you today.' He sounded annoyed himself and Paula wasn't missing anything at all; her face was tragic.

'Two o'clock,' Kip said tersely, glancing over his shoulder, and then he walked off with every line of his body showing temper.

'He dotes on you,' Ray observed wickedly, his eyes keenly on Neil's face. 'He's terrified something will happen to you.'

It was obvious what he was doing and Natalie was totally fed up with being piggy-in-the-middle. She rounded on him with flashing green eyes.

'Look, just shut up and let's get going!' If she dared not say it to Kip at least she could take it out on Ray and his wide grin acknowledged it.

'Just an observation,' he quipped. 'Let's roll.'

As they drove over the dam, Kip's car was parked across the other side of the road. He had been careful to place himself well out of any possible shot, having seen Natalie's photographs, but he was watching them all the same and Natalie tried her level best to look as if she wasn't standing up in the back.

Paula was driving and Neil was working out his commentary, which would be superimposed later in the studio. He might as well have stayed behind today, Natalie thought bitterly. He liked to be on the spot, though, to get the most out of the commentary, and after all he was supposed to be producing this.

She carefully held the boom clear of the camera, picking up the sound of the dam, lifting it to catch the sound of a bird that screeched in the air high above them and then lowering it again. It was hard work and needed care but all the same she seemed to see Kip's eyes burning into her angrily as they passed and it took all her resolution not to simply gaze back at him as tragically as Paula was looking this morning.

By the time two o'clock came around they were well on their way. Natalie and Ray were used to working together; they also had a very friendly working relationship, and Natalie was pleased to have as little as possible to do with Neil. Today if he so much as spoke out of turn she didn't know how she was going to hold her tongue.

Of course, having done very little, he grumbled that they had to break off to interview Kip, and Natalie could see trouble brewing there. Kip was not the sort of man to shrug any churlishness off as just one of those things. If Neil couldn't pull himself together and act with his customary smiling skill then Kip would simply walk off and leave them to it—end of interview.

'He's jealous,' Ray pointed out when she muttered her fears to him. 'Our boy likes to have his cake and eat it too. It's making him wild to see you with Kip Forsythe.'

'There's nothing between us,' Natalie protested, but he simply looked at her scathingly and did some muttering of his own.

'Then you're crazy. If I wanted you in bed as much as he does I'd drag you there by the hair.'

'For heaven's sake!' Natalie blushed bright red and Ray leered in satisfaction.

'The trouble with you, Natalie, is that you never grew up. The world is different now from the days of Grandma. Grasp your happiness while you can.'

'And the same to you,' Natalie said tartly.

'My happiness is engaged,' he murmured, his wicked smile dying, and she felt simply awful and mean.

'Oh, I'm sorry, Ray. I wish we'd never come out here.'

'An oversimplified solution. I'm staring my problem in the face daily. The venue isn't significant.'

Somehow it shocked her into comparing happiness with happiness. If Kip didn't love her, at least he wanted her. She had no doubt at all about that and, against all her instincts, she believed him about Annette. Ray was daily facing his torture. She should be more light-hearted about things. At least she could be pleasant to Kip. She was happy enough in his company if she could just control the urge to throw herself into his arms. They even talked the same language, liked the same things, both being devoted to their work.

Her new reflections showed on her face when they met him for the interview, and she had already planned that, to get the maximum impact out of it.

'I thought if we started with Kip standing against the dam and then cut to the actual workings of the dam we could kill two birds with one stone,' she said brightly, smiling at Kip, to his utter mystification.

His eyes narrowed and no doubt he was busily working out what she was up to but she saw his lips quirk with an amusement that was reflected in his eyes and she knew he had not the slightest qualm that whatever she threw at him he could handle.

'Perhaps I could plan my own interview?' Neil asked in exasperation. 'I would have thought you could sit back a bit now, Natalie. You've more or less managed us out of our minds.'

Natalie flushed at his reprimand but Ray was there before she could speak.

'And how lucky for some of us who left our minds in bed this morning,' he rasped. 'Natalie's worked like a slave. It's not either easy nor safe at the back of his vehicle.'

Her eyes met Kip's and she suddenly found herself looking down at her toes like a schoolgirl. Had he been saving a refusal until the last minute? She wouldn't put it past him. Apparently, though, he was prepared to back her up.

'I agree with Natalie,' he said coolly. 'There's a limit to what you can say about the surface of a dam. I'm pretty much at home among the turbines.' Neil looked about to say something unforgivable but Kip took matters out of his hands.

'Let me see your questions,' he ordered.

Natalie looked up at him with a sort of awed gratitude. It would take some sort of suicidal desire on Neil's part to buck against Kip, and Neil was a television man first and last. He swallowed his temper and settled to the discussion.

'Right. I'll talk around that,' Kip agreed shortly, and that was that.

He was so easygoing in front of the camera that Natalie and Ray had no problems at all, and even Neil relaxed into his old manner. Down in the workings of the dam Kip fascinated them so much that Ray almost forgot to keep the camera rolling. It was exciting, brilliantly so, watching Kip's dark eyes, the changing expressions on his face, his wonderful dark voice. The lean, tanned hands moved expressively, everything about him assured and elegant.

Later Ray admitted that he had hardly turned the camera on Neil at all.

'Kip should be in the movies,' he enthused. 'What a magnificent face—and the grand manner, so natural.' He grinned at Natalie. 'Excites you, doesn't he? I nearly dropped the damned camera when you took over so fervently.'

Natalie blushed. She could hardly forget it. She knew perfection when she saw it and she knew when to stop. Neil had been well into his stride, charmed by the sound of his own good voice, and he threw plenty of questions at Kip that had never even been mentioned. Kip hadn't turned a hair, although Natalie had wondered where Neil had got the sudden ideas. It would not have helped if Kip had floundered, although he didn't at all. He knew his work well.

It had been going on too long, though. She knew it instinctively and finally, after one of Kip's swift thrusts of humour that had them all grinning, she had been able to contain herself no longer. It was the perfect ending.

'Cut! We've got a wrap up!' She had just yelled it, banging Ray on the shoulder, getting instant obedience.

Neil had turned on her with a great deal of spiteful anger.

'Look! If you want to do everything just let me know and the rest of us will go home!'

'I'm sorry,' Natalie had murmured, trying to look placating. 'It was a perfect ending. I got carried away.' She had looked at Kip ruefully. 'Did you want to say anything else?'

'Not me.' He had grinned at her, the Kip she remembered, his laughing eyes almost warming her. He had glanced at his watch. 'Can the team take time off for tea?' he had enquired so pleasantly that even Neil's face had relaxed from rage. For a while, Kip had spoken to him with such charm that everything was smoothed over.

'Thanks,' Natalie murmured a moment later as they walked into the hotel for tea. 'I overstepped myself there.'

'I'm damned glad you did,' Kip said in a low voice. 'My smile was beginning to freeze.'

'You were simply wonderful,' Natalie assured him innocently, and he took her hand, looking down at her with sudden seriousness.

'Tell me that without all these people around us and I'll try my best to live up to it.'

For a second she seemed to be swimming in light, unable to look away, and Ray's words came so clearly back into her head, about grasping happiness. She would be grasping despair too, because she couldn't face any day afterwards if she gave herself to Kip and then had to forget him. As it was she would never, ever be able to forget him.

The Tamberi Falls took up the rest of the day. The sight of them stopped any sort of bickering. Knowing the terrain, Natalie made no mistake this time, and the other two stood in absolute awe, looking at the falls as she and Ray got the whole scene on to film.

'Well, that's it then,' Ray remarked as they all went back to the hotel. 'End of a perfect day.'

As far as Natalie was concerned it was anything but that. Still, the worst was over. Filming the official opening would be easy, barring unforeseen circumstances, although there had been plenty of those since she came here.

Neil had lived through his hangover and now he was looking at her with regret.

'Natalie, I'm sorry about this morning,' he said quietly when they were alone for a second. Paula had gone off to her room, misery still on her face, and it was clear to Natalie that if Ray stayed it would be to do what he had threatened before: poke Neil on the nose.

'Forget it,' she said easily. 'it's over and done with. Tomorrow should be easier.'

'What happened to us, Natalie, love?' he suddenly asked. 'Why did we let each other go?'

'As I recall, you got engaged.' She had been dreading this since they had come out here and she decided to take it lightly. He had no such idea, though. His face was set in grim lines.

'And I must have been out of my mind. I loved you from the moment I saw you.'

'That's enough, Neil!' Natalie said sharply. 'I don't know what you've got in mind but it's "no go". I happen to like Paula a lot.'

'So do I,' he muttered miserably. 'Who doesn't? The trouble is, she can't compare with you.'

She was saved a reply as a waiter came and murmured that she was wanted on the telephone. 'Mr Forsythe,' he informed her with all the deference that seemed to come at the sound of Kip's name.

'What does he want?' As she rose to leave, Neil grabbed her arm.

'Business, I expect.' She pulled free but Neil got to his feet, rage on his face.

'You sleep with him, don't you? I could see by the way he touched you even today that he owns you.'

Natalie stopped and looked at him with eyes colder than he had ever seen, emerald-green and sparkling with anger.

'Keep out of my affairs,' she warned in a low, angry voice. 'If this is anything to do with the film I'll tell you; if not, it's private. What Kip and I do is no concern of yours. You made your choice and I've made mine.'

What a stupid thing to say, she admonished herself as she walked off, leaving him staring after her. She hadn't made any choice at all. All she knew was that Paula had got herself engaged to a heel and if she had been given *that* choice herself it would have lasted about a week.

'Come to dinner with me,' Kip said as soon as he heard her voice.

'I can't.' Defence sprang instantly to her lips and mind.

'Then I'll not tell you my secret,' he answered breezily as if he couldn't care less whether she came or not.

'So keep it to yourself.' In spite of everything she was laughing and he knew it.

'Even if it's to do with the film?' he enquired ironically, knowing that would get her going. It did.

'Oh, Kip! Please tell me.'

'Wonderful. I love to hear you plead. I'll tell you over dinner, which Josh is now preparing.'

'This,' Natalie declared, 'is blackmail!'

'Take it or leave it,' he suggested.

'What time?'

'Seven? Shall I fetch you?' There was no sound of triumph in his voice but she could just imagine his laughing eyes.

'No fear. I'll bring my own transport.'

'In case you have to make a run for it.'

'You've got it,' Natalie applauded, grinning widely as she put the phone down. Ray and Paula had reappeared as she went back into the hotel lounge and she smiled brightly at all of them.

'Sorry, gang. I'm going out to dinner.'

'Business or pleasure?' Ray asked, unable to stop goading Neil, who looked white about the lips.

'A little of both. I'm going to Kip's house.'

'I'm surprised he didn't invite us all,' Neil snapped, but Ray got the last word in.

'If he had, I for one would have refused. I've never thought much of the idea of playing gooseberry.'

Kip was standing on the steps when she got there and she burst out of the car eagerly.

'What is it?' She was all eyes, vividly beautiful in a slip of a dress with a camisole top, its golden colour shimmering in the lights of the veranda.

'Maybe you won't like it.' Kip looked at her doubtfully and she had a bad moment before she saw his eyes glittering with amusement.

'Don't *tease* me!'

He took her arm, smiling down at her as he led her into the lighted lounge. 'Honestly, I can't seem to stop. You're the most entertaining girl when you're outraged. Speaking of which, I was very impressed by your performance today. If you could just keep yourself out of trouble, you'd go far.'

'But I am going far,' Natalie said pertly, looking up at him. 'The day after tomorrow we fly home—early.'

He looked down at her, his dark eyes speculating, and she took a small uneven breath. She didn't just love him, he was perfection to her; he had been since the first moment she had seen him. Everything about him brought her to singing life, his voice, his looks, the things he said . . .

'Stay another day,' he suggested softly, his eyes never leaving hers.

'I can't. You know I can't.'

He walked across and poured her a drink, turning to look back at her. 'Not even to interview Kane Mallory and get him on film?'

That stopped her in her tracks. She stared at him, her beautiful face animated.

'You're thinking,' Kip murmured. 'I can see your brain working. Dare you give up the chance of interviewing the boss? On the other hand, dare you face me for another day? You've got a problem.'

'It's no problem,' Natalie assured him quickly, her face flushing under his probing stare. 'Are you sure he's coming? Will he give an interview? Is he flying all the way from Canada?'

He came to hand her the drink but she put it firmly on the table, taking his and putting it there too, to his instant amusement.

'Wait! I've got to have more information. How do you know and——?'

'I knew he would be in England. He and Andrea are visiting Aunt Maureen. They have a house close by where they stay for a few months every year. I phoned him last night and found he was flying out for the opening in any case. After I did a little coaxing, he'll be delighted to give an interview. Well, knowing Kane, perhaps not delighted but willing. He'll not let you down—if you're interested.'

He smiled down into her enthusiastic face and she acted completely out of character. She flung her arms around his neck and tried her best to give him a hug.

'Oh, Kip! Thank you!' Just as his arms were tightening she spun away. 'I've got to let the others know. Can I use the phone?'

She didn't wait for permission and in minutes she had Neil on the phone, stopping his anxious enquiries with a rush of information.

'I'm sorry it's such short notice but I know you'll come up with some good ideas,' she wheedled.

'Are you coming back now?' His voice was strained and she felt her smile dying.

'You know I'm having dinner with Kip.' At the sound of her altered tone, Kip put his drink down and walked over to her.

'You'll come back early, of course?' Neil persisted. 'You can help me to work out the interview.'

Very amusing, considering his words this morning. She had no doubt at all about what he was intending.

'I could come back early,' she began and Kip's arms came round her from behind, slowly pulling her against him, his fair head bent to allow his lips to touch her hair. It just about settled everything and she felt her body sway towards him, curling into him like a sleepy child's.

'But I'm not coming back early,' she finished breathlessly, and Kip took the phone from her suddenly nerveless fingers, placing it back on the rest and turning her into his arms.

He bent his head and kissed her slender throat, his words murmured against her skin.

'For once, you said the right thing. At this moment I'm quite prepared to fight for you.' He looked up, tilting her face, his eyes burning into hers. 'Tonight you're staying with me.'

'Because you got me an interview with Kane Mallory?'

For a second his eyes darkened, an angry flash at the back of them, but something about her expression calmed his ready temper.

'Is that why you're staying?'

She did not think to deny that she would stay and all her feelings were in her wide green eyes.

'No,' she whispered, and his lips moved over hers slowly and gently, hypnotising her, melting her very soul.

Her arms lifted, clinging to him as she surrendered to the slow drowsy passion, delighting in the way her body melted into him, her bones turning to liquid.

'Kip!' She murmured his name into his mouth and he lifted his head, holding her close, rocking her against him, everything about him soothing, almost tender.

'We'd better have dinner, I think,' he whispered. 'I imagine Josh will come bursting in here at any moment to announce it.'

He led her through to the dining-room where the table had been set with more skill then Josh had previously shown.

'Mina,' Kip told her as she looked up in astonishment at the sight of the bowls of flowers, the glittering candles. 'I told her you were coming. She's fond of you.'

'More fond than she is of...' Suddenly her voice choked. She was already seated, Kip easing her chair in, and at the unhappy sound he tilted her face back, covering her mouth with his.

'Don't,' he said softly, his lips stroking hers. 'I would never let you be hurt, my beautiful Natalie.'

Perhaps he wouldn't, not deliberately, but then he didn't know how she felt. He didn't know she was clinging on to this night as if it were her last on earth. She twisted round, offering her lips completely, and his hands cupped her face with warm possession as he took the sweetness she offered. Only Josh stopped the long kiss and when Kip sat down opposite she was trembling uncontrollably, deeply aroused, her feelings made worse by the look in his eyes. He wanted her so much that his eyes were dazed. No man had ever looked at her like that before and no one would ever look at her like that again. It was Kip or no one at all for the rest of her life.

CHAPTER NINE

THEY talked about Kip's job, about Kane Mallory and the things he was likely to say.

'Not much,' Kip warned. 'Tell Bradshaw not to push it. If he behaves to Kane as he wanted to behave to me this afternoon he'll end up in the dam. Kane's not long on patience and he's got the devil of a temper.'

'You kept yours this afternoon,' Natalie pointed out softly. 'He managed to control himself. Thank you.'

'You know why I was prepared to smooth him over,' Kip said, his eyes darkly intent on her. There was so much feeling in his gaze that she looked away, her thick lashes screening her eyes as her head bent.

'I fully expect Kane's going to arrive with my next job all lined up.' Kip changed the subject smoothly, easing the tension but Natalie's head shot up, pain shooting through her. He might be right across the world. She would never see him again.

'Where? Have you any idea?'

'I've a distinct feeling it may be South America. He mentioned it when I phoned and I know there's a lot brewing there for Mallory-Carter.'

'All those *señoritas*,' Natalie managed with a trembling smile.

For a minute his eyes probed her mind, the lids narrowing over the glowing dark. 'Tell me about Bradshaw,' he suddenly demanded. He looked different, harsh, no laughter glittering in his eyes at all, and Natalie felt uneasy, almost as if she were pinned like a

154

real butterfly, struggling to escape inspection by a cold, interested gaze. There was even the hint of cruelty, something she had never seen before, and she dared not lie.

'He joined Westwind about eighteen months ago. Before that he was a sort of big-shot producer. I could never understand why he came to us.'

'Did you know him before?'

'I'd met him, yes.'

'You're weaving neatly around the main question,' Kip said curtly. 'You know what I'm asking, Natalie.'

'I went out with him for about a year.' Suddenly she was resentful, not scared any more, and her green eyes flashed angrily. 'Have you the information you want now?'

'I think so.' He leaned back, cradling his coffee-cup in his hands. Josh had cleared the rest of the dishes and she knew his style. He would be off now to his little bungalow, joining Mina in front of a television that never seemed to be switched off, the coffee-cups left for morning. The house seemed uncannily silent.

'So he's the one who hurt you,' Kip said flatly. 'Paula drifted on to the scene. He's not making her very happy.'

'Is that *my* fault?' Natalie felt as if she was choking. From gentle, coaxing kisses he had turned into a cold, clinical interrogator.

'He'd ditch her tomorrow if he could have you back.' He watched her intently. 'Can he have you back, Natalie?'

'Well, he can have me back tonight to help with tomorrow's interview!' She stood and gathered her little bag, moving to the veranda before he could stop her. He was there immediately but he did not need to take any action. As she reached the veranda the heavens seemed to open with no warning at all. Rain came in a deluge, thunder rolled like a gigantic drum, lightning crackled across the black sky and she stopped in her tracks, a small sound of alarm in her throat.

'Even the gods are against you,' Kip said drily behind her. 'They're no more prepared to let you go than I am.'

She turned in bewilderment to look at him. He was outlined against the light, tall, powerful and thrilling. Tears sprang into her eyes and she bit down on her lip, shaking her head in a small gesture of despair when his hands came to her shoulders.

'What am I, Natalie?' he asked harshly. 'A consolation prize? I never have been willing to be second choice in anything.'

'There's no choice,' she whispered shakily. 'Neil and I, we just work together.'

'And fight. What is that about, frustration? His or yours?'

Suddenly she went mad, lashing out at him in a flare of loving and hating that tore into her.

'You don't know me! What do you know about me? Nothing!' Her fists began to pummel his broad chest and he just let her go on, keeping her locked inside the circle of his arms as she wore herself out. 'Am I to blame because he's tired of Paula? I hate men—all men! I hate *you*!'

He bent his head and cut off the unhappy rage, taking her mouth so violently that her breath threatened to stop. There was anger and frustration in both of them and a rising excitement that made her legs go weak. He ravaged her mouth, his hands on her body anything but gentle. He was angry. She could feel it surging through him but, all the same, she was where she wanted to be and the bitterness died inside her as swiftly as it had come.

She softened against him, not fighting any more, and he felt the surrender ripple through her. His harsh grip eased, the fierce tension in his body changing from anger to desire, but there was still a sort of thrilling tyranny, a demand for submission. His arms were like iron, every muscle taut, and the hand that gripped her head, holding it up to his, was a cradle of steel.

'Kip!' She tore her lips away, scared and excited, trembling, tremors running through her voice, but he grasped her head, forcing her back to him, his mouth open over hers.

'Be still!' It was a harsh command, his eyes glittering down at her. 'I've no desire at all to hurt you.'

'I don't care.' Her lips brushed his and he stiffened at her whispered confession.

'Little fool! There are more ways than one of devouring you.'

Suddenly he was gentle, her shivering body folded in his arms, his hand soothing her nape beneath the heavy, long hair. A few feet beyond them, outside the shelter of the veranda, the rain fell in a torrent, as if it would never stop, and she wished it would rain forever, trapping her here with Kip, trapping him in her life.

When he lifted her and walked inside, slamming the door closed behind them, she saw nothing of the room. A weight seemed to be on her eyelids, her lashes brushing her tinted cheeks, and he looked down at her with harsh, masculine desire. Slender, her body no burden at all to his strength, she lay in his arms like a vivid flower, her shimmering golden dress, her long black hair that cascaded over his arm adding a radiance to her that was unreal. Black and gold as he had first seen her, a mixture of fragility and defiance, anger and submission, she was now completely lost, unable and unwilling to fight him.

His eyes narrowed over her face as he slid her to the
floor in his bedroom. Suddenly she looked like a beautiful sacrifice, but the drive to own her was un-
quenchable. At this moment she was in his bloodstream
and she would have to beg him to let her go. He wanted
her with an intensity he had never felt before.

Natalie was not begging. As his arms left her, she
swayed towards him, resting against the strength of his
chest, and he cupped her face with warm hands, making
her meet his eyes.

'You want me to take you to bed?' A last ray of sanity
forced him to ask, and delicate colour rushed under her
skin, her lashes drifting down to cover her eyes.

'Shall I beg?' Her voice trembled and he caught her
to him fiercely.

'From me? Never that, not with you!'

He was stirred at once, crushing her against him, his
mouth searching hers deeply and endlessly as his hands
caressed her body with growing desperation. When he
slid her dress away she was naked to the waist, her breasts
taut beneath his hands, and he bent his head to fondle
them with urgent lips as Natalie's fingers unfastened his
shirt, her breathing fast and uneven at the thought of
his skin once again on hers.

'Please, Kip! Please, please love me,' she begged in a
small broken voice and he lifted her to the bed, his eyes
blazing down at her as he finished undressing both of
them.

When he came to her, pulling her close, her name was
a jagged sound in his throat.

'*Natalie!*' He rained kisses all over her, unable to think
beyond this one moment, his hands stroking the whole
of her skin, his kisses more deep and intimate each

second until she was sobbing in his arms, wild tears in her eyes.

He kissed them away, her own desperation inside him.

'If you leave me now, it will kill me,' he groaned. 'I can't wait for you, Natalie!'

He possessed her with fierce tenderness, his mouth crushing the wild cry that rose in her throat, his hands holding her fast when pain speared through her. And then the pain was gone, the feeling of almost frightening pleasure spinning her into another world where Kip's arms held her securely, a world that Kip entered too, never leaving her until they drifted back to the lamplit room together.

He was heavy over her, his body still shuddering in the aftermath of passion, and she lifted a trembling hand and stroked the fair head that lay against her breast. Dark eyes looked up at her and he raised himself to look down into her face, seeing the glitter of tears. It filled him with remorse, his hand touching her soft cheek.

'I hurt you and you cried.' His eyes darkened further as he saw fresh tears flood to the surface. 'Don't, baby,' he pleaded. He swallowed hard and she managed to smile, her arms looping around his neck.

It had nothing to do with pain, this desolate feeling that seemed to come from the very centre of her being. Soon he would be gone; so would she. She would never see him again. And what was she? One of his loves— for one night.

'Kip.' She whispered his name and he rolled to his side, crushing her against him.

'Don't leave me,' he ordered. 'Don't leave me for even a second. I'll come after you across the world.'

If only that were true. She curled against him, arching readily at the stroking of his hands until his eyes

questioned hers and she melted back into his hard
warmth, a beautiful, pliant being with no desire to ever
leave this night behind.

In the early morning Natalie awoke, gently easing
herself from the arms that held her tightly. For one night
there had been love, endless love, and now the sun would
soon rise on a new day, a day fresh and golden, the green
of the trees and grass brilliant after the rain that had
lasted most of the night.

Kip lay sleeping, his face relaxed, a half-smile on his
lips, and she couldn't resist dropping a kiss on his mouth
before she got carefully out of bed and slid her arms
into his shirt, wrapping it around her and walking to the
window.

As she opened it the song of a bird startled her. It was
a clear, melodious sound, three falling notes repeated
three times and then four notes following with quick-
ening rhythm. It was beautiful, eerie, sad but joyous.
She was held spellbound listening.

'The joy of the morning. A hymn to the beauty after
rain.'

Kip's arms came round her from behind. He had
slipped into a robe without her having heard his movements and he pulled her back against him.

'What is it?' She leaned back, looking up into his eyes,
and he smiled down at her.

'An ornithologist I most certainly am not,' he
confessed, his lips trailing over her cheeks. 'However, I
can tell you what *we* call it. You're listening to the rain
bird.'

'Where is it?' Her eyes searched the trees in the
gathering light and he pointed beyond her.

'Somewhere in that tree. It seems to have one favourite
spot. You can't see it from here and in any case it's

nothing spectacular, a small black and white bird you'd never notice until it sings.'

'After the rain?'

'Always after the rain,' he confirmed softly. 'It always seems to know something we don't know at all.'

Did it know her despair? Did it know that she too felt the same joy and sadness? She shivered with an uncanny feeling of predestiny and Kip turned her away, lifting her against him.

'You're cold. Come back to bed. It will soon be morning and I'll lose you.' How readily he said it, but how she needed him. She turned into his arms as he placed her back in the warm bed and his lips were instantly tender and demanding.

It was after breakfast before she got back to the hotel and the others were standing on the steps, looking at the bright morning. There was no doubt at all where she had spent the night. She still wore the golden dress, the dainty sandals, her evening bag in her hand when she turned to lock the car. Her face was transformed, serene but haunted, and Neil pounced on her regardless of the others.

'Where the hell have you been?'

'Don't you remember? I went out to dinner.'

'And stayed with him all night.'

'Maybe I didn't bother to change this morning,' Natalie snapped. Really, she wasn't up to this. She felt she would never be up to anything else ever again.

'You weren't in your room all night!' He stared at her furiously and Natalie's face froze. Behind him she could see Paula and Ray. She had no idea if they could hear or not.

'And how would you know that?'

Something about her tone warned him that he was stepping into danger and he stepped back, getting control of the anger that made him ugly.

'I kept calling. There's this damned new interview you set up for today.'

'And since when have you either needed or welcomed my help on such things?' Natalie asked tightly. 'You've got until midday to work it out. Kane Mallory flies in at eleven and the official opening is at three. If you scrape in an interview after that we can leave as planned tomorrow.'

She spun round and left him standing there, smiling tightly at Ray and Paula as she passed. Up in her room she changed and showered. It was no use after all. Kip had wanted her to stay one more day. He had never even mentioned anything else. She might just as well go on the early flight tomorrow as they had planned. Her brief time with Kip was over almost before it had begun.

She didn't tell Neil that she was going with Kip to meet his sister and brother-in-law. She felt it would only provoke another outburst and when Kip's car drew up outside the hotel she was watching for him. She raced outside and slid in beside him almost before he had stopped.

'Where's the fire?' He leaned over and dropped a kiss on her mouth, surprising her by the old possessive sweetness. She almost told him then that she loved him. Instead she smiled up at him and began to question him about his sister.

'Will she be coming with him?'

'I imagine so. He's not likely to let her out of his sight and she's a persistent little devil.'

'She's small?' Natalie looked across with some surprise, in view of Kip's height, and he grinned to himself.

'Only in size. All the energy that didn't go into growing is packed inside and bursts out constantly. Andrea is a handful.'

Of course they did not arrive on a scheduled flight and Natalie wondered why on earth she had imagined they would. Kane Mallory was a millionaire many times over. A silver executive jet touched down within minutes of their arrival and taxied to the edge of the tarmac.

'Punctual as ever.' Kip glanced at his watch and then grinned to himself as one of the most powerful-looking men that Natalie had ever seen swung to the ground. He raised a hand casually to Kip and strange golden eyes flared briefly over Natalie. Then he was reaching inside, helping out his wife, Kip's sister, and Natalie's green eyes really *did* open wide.

Andrea Mallory was the smallest, prettiest thing that Natalie had ever seen. Her dark eyes were exactly like Kip's but her hair was spun silver. She broke away from her husband's restraining arms and simply flew at Kip, flinging herself at him and being swung off her feet in a great bear-hug.

'Ease off, Kip. We're pregnant.'

Kane Mallory was beside them in two strides, detaching his wife from Kip's embrace and tucking her neatly under his shoulder.

'Again?' Kip grinned into her flushed face. 'Where's Suzy?'

'With Aunt Maureen. Oh, I do hope we have a boy this time. I know Kane wants one.'

'Girls are just fine.' He smiled down at her and then turned his attention to Natalie, the golden eyes summing her up swiftly. 'I hope you're not here to interview me right now, young lady. I've got a lot of business to talk over with Kip first.

'She's with me,' Kip assured him, his hand coming to Natalie's arm in a way that brought instant interest to Andrea Mallory's eyes and a faint flush to Natalie's cheeks. 'I might remind you too that the official opening is at three.'

'And the interview?' Once more Natalie got the benefit of the strange tawny glance and held herself a little stiffly.

'After the opening, if you can manage it.'

'Don't be scared of him,' Andrea advised with a grin. 'He's not nearly as bad as he looks.'

She got an amused, chiding look from the big man, who almost lifted her into the waiting car before piling their two suitcases into the back.

'Why this afternoon?' Kip held Natalie back and spoke in a low voice. 'I thought it was tomorrow.'

'If he'll do it today we can keep to our schedule.' She hardly dared look at him and she could almost feel the waves of anger that flew across his face.

'Just like that,' he said flatly.

'We're on a tight schedule. You know that.' What did he expect? How was she supposed to cope with things? Already the bottom had dropped out of her world. One more night—was that what he was offering? He didn't speak to her again. Somehow he contained his anger and managed to hold an ordinary conversation with his two visitors but once or twice Natalie caught Andrea's eyes on her through the rear-view mirror, puzzled and speculating. No doubt she knew her own brother.

The official opening was indeed spectacular. The road across the dam was closed, the one or two cars that needed to cross being manoeuvred slowly by the police. While they had been at the airport seating had been arranged and a heavy ribbon in the blue, red and amber of the Madembi flag was fastened across the road, ready for the minister to cut.

The Kabala Hotel too was a hive of industrious activity, the dining-room cleared for the official dance that the minister had ordered. Lunch was a buffet in the lounge, and who cared about lunch when this day was so important? The waiters' grins said it all.

As his visitors went off to their rooms, Kip held Natalie back, his fingers flexing on her arm.

'Right now I have to go, but after the opening you and I talk.' He sounded particularly grim, not a smile in sight, and after the way he had not spoken to her on the drive from the airport Natalie was tightly wound up with anger and misery.

'What have we got to talk about?' She glanced at him defiantly and then dropped her eyes as his face flared with temper.

'If you don't know, then maybe we have nothing to talk about after all,' he bit out. She noticed his glance flash to Neil who was watching them as closely as ever and her own temper rose. What exactly was she in all this masculine rivalry? Not good enough to be engaged to Neil, nothing more than a night's love-affair with Kip.

She spun away from him and ran up to her room, temper sustaining her until she got there, her eyes filling with tears as soon as the door was safely closed. She had to get through this day, that was all. Tomorrow night she would be back in London and Kip would simply take up his life where he had left off, expecting her to do the same.

As to Neil, she had already decided about that. She would leave Westwind, get away from the studio. In her travels she had seen many things, taken hundreds of excellent photographs. She had about a trunkful of notes and she would write. Maybe Paula would see some sense and leave Neil, but whether she did or not Natalie was certain that *she* would not be the one to cause the break-up. She could not see now why she had ever been taken in by Neil. Kip filled her every thought, her whole existence—hopelessly.

The minister sat with his wife in the centre. To one side sat Kane and Andrea Mallory and at the other side of him Kip, frowning and dangerous-looking, like a fair-haired bandit in expensive clothes, as Ray put it. The other government officials took up the rest of the front row and as she moved with Ray, working the sound, Natalie found her eyes searching for Annette; after all, wasn't Annette a fairly important person in these parts? She had set up the school from nothing, as she had already told Natalie.

She was there, of course, her face carefully composed, and Natalie almost laughed aloud; Annette dared not glare in case the camera caught her.

'Lord! The mad sorceress!' Ray muttered from behind the camera as he panned the crowd. 'If she's in the film, I'll cut it.'

'For heaven's sake be quiet,' Natalie whispered, looking worriedly at the microphone. 'And don't get me laughing.'

'Could anything do that?'

Right at the moment, she knew that nothing could.

All the same, she had to get into the swing of things. The interview with Kane Mallory went off perfectly. He had the sort of relaxed air in front of the camera that Kip had, although his eyes strayed frequently to his petite wife who never once looked away from him. It brought a lump to Natalie's throat. That was how she felt about Kip. She had to ignore him, though, because now that the ribbon had been cut and the crowd had begun to move to the hotel for refreshments Annette had claimed Kip and she was obviously waiting with bated breath to be introduced to Kane Mallory and his wife.

As soon as it was dark there were fireworks, all the guests going out to the front of the hotel to watch, and Natalie went with Ray. They stood looking as the coloured lights flared upwards into the velvet African sky and if it had not been for Kip, Natalie would have been well pleased. Her task was over, mission accomplished. She could go home.

A very familiar hand came to her arm and her skin shivered in recognition before Kip even spoke.

'Can I borrow the boss, Ray?' Natalie thought his voice was as dark as the night and her eyes met his with a flicker of anxiety as he turned her towards him at Ray's laughing agreement.

'My sister is very anxious to meet you again,' he informed Natalie as she hesitated, her whole body awash with panic. She could feel his hands on her body, his lips searching her skin. She wanted to cry out that it was unfair, impossible to live through, and he must have seen the turmoil on her face because his hand tightened, drawing her closer to his side.

'No outrageous scenes, Natalie,' he warned softly. 'Half the people here are looking at you.'

'Of course they're not.' She dropped her silky head, hiding her face. 'Why should they be?'

'Would you believe—because you're so damned beautiful?' A rhetorical question, and he wasn't waiting for any answer either. He drew her through the crowds to the inside and straight over to Andrea, whose dark eyes seemed to note everything, just like Kip's. She used the same method of interrogation too, straight out and no hesitation. She wanted to know all about Westwind and Natalie's job.

Kane joined them, his arm coming instantly around Andrea's waist, and Natalie almost had to stifle a cry. She felt lost and lonely, more lonely than she had ever felt in her life. It seemed ages before she could get away, muttering about having to check with her team that everything was finally wrapped up.

Annette caught her before she had reached the sanctuary of Ray's side.

'So you're finished and going?' The pale blue eyes snapped out at her and Natalie looked back with distaste.

'First thing in the morning,' she said curtly, not in any way wanting to chatter to this woman.

'Well, it must have been quite an experience for you. In a way, I suppose, I don't begrudge you it at all. There's a certain magic about Africa, and I knew you'd end up in Kip's bed, even though briefly. He's not a man to be denied.'

Cold shivered over Natalie's skin and she looked back carefully, controlling her voice with a great effort of will.

'I beg your pardon?'

'My dear! You stayed with Kip last night.'

'And where did you get that mad idea from?' Natalie choked.

'Well, Kip of course. He told me. Don't worry, it won't go any further. I'm the soul of discretion and he's been telling me his secrets since I came out here.' She shrugged easily. 'After all, who else is there in this place? And I did tell you we were always together. I'm not jealous. It's one of those things, a new face.'

Ray came up with some speed, seeing Natalie's tragic expression, an expression she couldn't hide at all. It said everything so very well. A new face to enliven the scene.

Ray took her arm tightly, his grip warming.

'Your broomstick just drew up outside, Annette,' he bit out, turning Natalie away as Annette's face flushed brightly.

'Well, I've never——' she began angrily but Ray had the last word as he turned.

'I'm sure you have. Every picture tells a story.'

He took Natalie off and led her to the foyer where there were few people about. 'Whatever she said,' he warned urgently, 'discount it. I pointed out the possibility of knives when we first encountered her. Kip's crazy about you.'

'No. I'm the one who's crazy,' Natalie murmured, half whispering. 'I knew the set-up. I just walked right into it. I'm going to bed, Ray.' She put her hand on his arm, looking up at him, her olive-tinted skin shockingly white. 'Thank you again. You've never stopped rescuing me since you came here. If there's anything I can ever do for you...'

'Kill Bradshaw,' he muttered as he left. 'Nothing else will do, kiddo.'

Natalie was trembling so much by the time she reached her room that she had to sit down. So that was all it had meant? He had told Annette already and she was quite prepared to take him back on the old terms.

Why had she believed him when he had said there was nothing between him and that woman? You didn't tell things like that to a casual acquaintance. She could hardly believe it of Kip but how else could Annette have known? In any case, hadn't she been forewarned? In love for one night at a time. Tears streamed down her face and she could still not stem them when someone knocked at the door.

She was wiping her eyes frantically as she opened it and the sight of Neil standing there almost had her slamming it in his face.

'What do you want?' She almost screamed it and he looked completely shocked, coming in before she could stop him and pushing the door to.

'For God's sake, Natalie! You're yelling.'

'Not as much as I'd like to be.' She turned her back and rubbed at her eyes, trying to gather some composure round her before she faced him. She took a deep breath and spun round.

'What can I do for you?' It was difficult to control her voice but she did it and his face softened, making him look like the Neil she had imagined him to be. It seemed a long time ago now.

'Come back down to the party, Natalie. Stay with me. I know you're unhappy and I can't bear to see it.'

'Thank you,' she managed, not able to keep the sarcasm from her voice. 'How kind everyone is being to me.'

'There's no kindness in Forsythe,' he said tightly. 'I tried to warn you, darling, but you always have been headstrong.'

Darling! He really didn't know when to quit! Natalie's eyes narrowed to glittering green but he was beside her before she could speak, his arms coming round her tightly as he grabbed her with a show of desperation that took her breath away.

'Let me *go*!'

'No, darling, no. I know how I've hurt you, why you turned to Forsythe.' He began to scatter kisses all over her face, holding her fast when she struggled. 'We'll go back to London and be together again. Paula will understand. Deep down she knows it's you I love and she's a nice girl.'

'Too nice for a swine like you!' The cold, harsh voice from the doorway stopped Neil in his tracks and Natalie almost fell as he let her go abruptly and swung to face Kip.

'What are you doing here?' Neil sounded outraged as if he himself had every right to be here.

'Making a mistake, obviously,' Kip rasped, his eyes furiously on Natalie's flushed face. 'If you want rescuing, say so now,' he bit out, and it was quite enough to send her from misery into a rage. It was clear what he thought and why shouldn't he? He went from one woman to the next with skilful ease. To a man like that, every woman was the same.

'Out! Get out, both of you!' She stormed to the door and swung it open wide and Kip took one look at her rather ferocious face and turned on his heel, disgust written clearly in his eyes. Neil lingered, his hand stretched out to her. If he told her to calm down and not be an impetuous little thing she would kill him and fulfil Ray's wishes. She reached for the nearest ornament and handled it threateningly. 'Out!' There was not one flicker of compromise in her face and Neil went, murmuring that he would see her tomorrow when she had calmed down.

She locked the door firmly, threw herself on the bed and cried her eyes out.

CHAPTER TEN

EVERYTHING looked the same, Natalie thought. Her life was completely changed and yet London looked the same: the studio, her father, the house they had lived in for so many years. Nothing had changed except herself. The strain of putting the film together was enormous because there was no way she could get out of it. She had to sit there in the dark and help with the editing, forcing herself to watch Kip, listening to his voice. Once, in the darkness, Ray's hand covered hers and gave a helping squeeze, but in actual fact nothing helped. She loved Kip and she would always love him, whatever had happened.

The morning they had left Africa she had been over-quiet, dreading meeting him, fearing that he would come, but it had been Andrea who had come, knocking on her door as she was preparing to leave.

'Forgive me, Natalie,' she said quietly. 'I couldn't help noticing how upset you became last night. I can't let you go without speaking to you. It's Kip, isn't it?'

'Don't worry about me.' It was impossible to relax and smile, pretend that everything was all right. How many times had she said those words since she came out here? Don't worry about me.

'I'm worried about you both,' Andrea said doggedly. 'I love Kip very much. I've never seen him like this before. Last night he was almost violent.'

'Does everything *have* to be my fault?' Natalie asked bitterly, and much against her will tears sprang into her eyes.

'My dear, I'm so sorry. Can't you wait for him, another day?'

'There's absolutely nothing to wait for.' She had no doubt about that. If there had been, Kip would have been here now. He would have stayed last night and found out what was happening with Neil. He would never have told Annette about their night together. She couldn't bend, couldn't soften. If she did it would be the end of her and she would be crying her eyes out in front of this beautiful woman who had a husband who adored her.

They boarded the flight and she did not look round to see if Kip was there. He would not be there. He knew the time of the flight. It was all over and all she could do was gather her courage about her to face the journey home. Not that she was afraid this time. Somehow it didn't seem to matter.

With the film out of the way she tackled her father.

'I'm leaving Westwind. I'm also moving into a flat of my own.'

Nothing could have stopped him in his tracks more. For a second he just stared at her and then thundered, his normal way of behaving.

'I'm damned if you are,' he threatened. 'If this is Bradshaw then he can go—now!'

'It has nothing at all to do with Neil,' she persisted patiently. 'Firstly, I want to write. Secondly, I've grown scared of flying.'

'Rubbish!' He boomed at her and fixed her with a deadly eye, his sure winner. 'Since when has my daughter been scared of anything?'

'Since right now. It's no use carrying on like this. I've made my mind up.' It took a whole evening of insistence on Natalie's part and an unexpected willingness to 'plea bargain' on her father's before she won out. She could give it six months, he agreed. He was satisfied with that because he clearly thought she would be back. It settled his temper and satisfied his ego but Natalie knew she would not be back. She wanted a hole of her own, a corner to cry in, a place where she could work in peace and try to pull herself together.

It was bitterly cold for late autumn. Natalie looked round her new flat and felt a certain amount of satisfaction. As a hidey-hole, it wasn't bad. Even her father approved. After several visits, with him asking scathingly why her own home was no longer good enough for her, he had finally realised that neither sarcasm nor bullying would win her over.

She had decorated it herself, back-breaking work that had helped to take her mind off Kip. Ray had popped in once or twice to see her, scrupulously making no mention of either Kip or Neil. The film was due to be shown on television. He had slipped that bit of information in very carefully and, though she dreaded it, she knew she would watch. She wanted to see Kip again. Time had not eased things. Still, it was only a matter of weeks. One day the ache would go. It would have to.

She put all the furniture back in place and looked round in satisfaction. Everything looked good. Tomorrow she would really start to work but it would be a long time before she would dare to tackle her book on Madembi. She wouldn't even write an article about it.

Going into the bathroom to wash her hands, she suddenly found herself feeling faint, bending over the sink, everything swimming before her eyes. Nausea washed over her and for a few minutes she was very ill, only just hearing the doorbell ring. She had hardly managed to wipe her face and take a careful look at herself in the mirror before it rang again so insistently that she just knew it was her father. Patience was not his strong point and he never had liked to be kept waiting.

'Sorry.' She opened the door and found him glaring down at her. 'I—er—was in the bathroom.'

'No hurry,' he muttered, looking at her suspiciously. 'Just called to see how things were.'

She hid a little smile. He hadn't done anything of the sort. He was almost constantly here and she knew why. He was hoping to wheedle her back to Westwind. A man had taken her place and, according to Ray, her father was already thinking of strangling him. It was a boost to her ego but nothing would get her back. She had some healing to do and she could do it much better here.

'Place looks good. I miss you, of course.' He turned and glared at her affectionately. 'But I can see that you'd want a place of your own at your age.'

'In my dotage, you mean?' Natalie said, grinning at him, waiting for the next bit.

'You know what I mean. You're a woman.'

'Gosh!' Natalie laughed aloud.

'No reason why you have to live at home,' he conceded. 'Now that you've got this place set up you can come back to Westwind.'

'No deal!' Natalie said firmly. 'I've told you what I intend to do.'

He never had the chance to reply because the nausea washed over her again and she raced for the bathroom.

When she lifted her head, her father was there, wiping her face and then almost carrying her back to sit on the settee. She had never known him be so gentle and, glancing up, she had to admit she also had never seen him in quite such a rage.

'You're pregnant!' He looked just about ready to explode and she opened her mouth to correct him, utterly astonished at his conclusions. 'Don't bother to say anything,' he roared. 'I knew there was something. Since you came back from Madembi you've looked haunted, tormented. Is this why you've left and moved from home?'

'I am not pregnant!' Natalie retaliated hotly, knowing for sure that she wasn't. 'You know damned well I had a virus in Africa. This is just the same in many ways. I'll go to the doctor tomorrow.'

She might as well have kept silent. Nobody corrected Jonas West because he was never wrong.

'It's Bradshaw!' he pronounced, towering over her. 'The dog! Decided he likes you best after all, has he? I'll break his neck!'

He was already at the door when Natalie reached him, grabbing his arm.

'I'm not *pregnant*!' she shouted, the only way to get through to him when he was like this.

'The hell you *are*. I've seen your mother like this. I'm not an idiot.'

'Well, you could have fooled me. Just calm down and listen to me. This is a virus.'

'One that's going to last nine months. Bradshaw goes. If he's lucky I'll only slightly maim him.' He turned and thrust an angry finger at her. 'You're not marrying him, you hear me, girl?'

'I have no intention of marrying him,' Natalie raged. 'And I'm *not* pregnant——'

He slammed the door and she dived to the phone. Neil might be all sorts of a rat but she felt the need to warn him. The line was engaged. She tried for the next hour but still got no answer. It was all too late then. Her father would be back at the studio, if he hadn't been imprisoned for reckless driving. It was just so ridiculous and she was soon too sick to bother anyway.

'I've sacked him.' Her father rang in the evening, his temper somewhat under control. 'He denied it but I sacked him anyway.'

'You,' Natalie said, not knowing whether to laugh or cry, 'are a bad man.'

'Be that as it may,' he grunted. 'You're my own. I'll see you through this.'

'Thank you so much,' she said sweetly. 'You can keep handing me glasses of water to take my penicillin capsules. I've had the doctor and he assures me that your future grandson is nothing more than a virus.'

It shut him up but not for more than a second.

'If you're lying I'll know finally,' he said with a smugness that seemed to him to cancel out all his sins. 'As for Bradshaw, I couldn't stand him, never could, even when you were going out with him. That poor kid Paula was in tears this afternoon.'

'Are you surprised? You monster.'

'She should get rid of him. He's a wimp in disguise,' he said firmly, putting the phone down and leaving Natalie open-mouthed. She could imagine what sort of a scene there had been at the studio. There was nothing her father liked better than a good scene either on or off film.

The next day Ray called round to tell her all about it, his face creased with laughter.

'If you could possibly come back now, love,' he said after he had related the disgraceful affair, 'I'd be grateful. With Bradshaw gone I might just be the next in line because there's always got to be somebody to get under your father's feet.'

'Wild horses wouldn't drag me back,' Natalie assured him. 'I'm not going to have to admit that my father's a clever lunatic. From now on everybody takes care of themselves and that, mate, includes you.'

He couldn't have been gone more than half an hour before the bell rang again and it was Paula, in tears.

'It was so awful, Natalie,' she sniffed after Natalie had settled her down with a cup of tea, assured yet another person that she was not pregnant and listened to the whole story all over again.

'The worst thing was that Neil wasn't angry about your father's accusations. Of course he hotly denied it but at one stage in the row he shouted that he wished it were true.'

'Dad should never have fired him,' Natalie said, biting her lip and wondering how she was going to reassure Paula about Neil after all this.

'Oh, he didn't.' Paula looked up at her with wide blue eyes. 'It was obvious that he was going to but Neil just left. On the spot. It was while he was clearing his desk out that I knew he still loved you, knew it for sure. He was white and shaking. He kept saying "It's that bastard Forsythe!" He wanted it to be *him*!'

She burst into tears again and Natalie sat beside her, putting her arms round the shaking shoulders. Right at that moment she could have done violence to her own father. Of course he would never have mentioned that

Neil had got his resignation in first. He had meant to sack him and, in his soaring ego, he had.

'What are you going to do about Neil?' she asked softly.

'Oh, I'd already decided that really,' Paula said shakily. 'I gave him his ring back last night. I'm not happy, Natalie, but Ray's been so good to me. Ray was nice to me in Madembi and I got to seeing just what Neil was like. It's lucky we went out there, isn't it?'

'It is,' Natalie said quietly, denying it inside with all her heart. If she had never been out to Madembi she would never have met Kip and she would not now be busy just trying to get through each day. By the time Paula left, she was exhausted. She went to bed. It was the night of the television showing of their film but she couldn't bear to face it.

She dreamed of Kip. She was in his arms, warmed by his love, and the song of the rain bird drifted hauntingly towards an African dawn. When she awoke, her pillow was wet with tears.

Natalie walked towards her flat along the quiet road. The bitter cold had eased but the wind still blew strongly, scattering the bright leaves of autumn around her, producing little whirlwinds of colour that swirled around her feet and then vanished. The virus had lasted nearly two weeks and had left her more slender than ever but today she was more at peace.

She had been to the studio to collect some of her photographs that had been stored there and she held the little parcel in her hand now. They had been delighted to see her. Paula had made coffee at once and the three of them had settled down for a chat, some subtle persuasion being used to get her back. It had failed, but her father, ever hopeful, had glanced at them keenly and gone off with unusual quiet, hoping for results.

The new man had taken an instant dislike to her and the feeling was mutual. She couldn't see him lasting long, which was a problem; already they were one member short. It gave her a pang of guilt but she knew it was now or never. If she went back, then she was never going to be able to strike out on her own, and it had become almost a matter of frantic importance.

Some days she managed to forget Kip for all of an hour. The nights were the worst times. When evening fell she could see nothing but his face, hear nothing but the haunting melody of the bird at dawn.

One good thing had come from all this misery. Paula and Ray seemed to be keeping steady company, as Ray put it with a happy grin. Paula was back as she had been, a bubbly little thing who looked too fluffy-headed to produce any work at all. It was funny how good came out of everything—except for her.

The man who sat in his car and watched her narrowed his eyes at the picture she made. She was too slender, the wind almost blowing her along, catching her long black hair and sweeping it around her too pale face. It moulded her coat to her, outlining her fragility, and his lips tightened for a minute before he quietly opened the door and stepped out into the cool air.

She stopped so suddenly that she seemed to have been caught by the wind, ready to be swept away into another little whirlwind of colour. Her pallor increased and she caught at her flying hair, holding it down against her shoulder.

'Why are you here?' Her voice was nothing more than a rush of trembling breath and he came to her quickly, fearing she would faint, his dark eyes intent on her face.

'To see you. Isn't that obvious?'

'Nothing is obvious.' Her green eyes flashed with some of the old spark and she swung away from him. 'You've seen me. Goodbye.'

Inside she was hurting so much that it was a major effort to keep her face still but she had learned a lot since she had first seen him and the one thing to know was when to get out.

'If you're going to make one of your little scenes we'll have it indoors, shall we?' He caught her arm, holding her more tightly when she tried to free herself.

'You're not coming in!' She wanted him to hold her close but she would never again allow herself that luxury.

'Give me your key.' When she refused to make a move he took her handbag without any hesitation, searching it impatiently.

'Somewhere among this hundredweight of equipment there's sure to be a key,' he murmured, finding it and inserting it into the lock with a certain amount of suppressed violence. 'Inside, Natalie, before you just blow away.'

Inside the flat he calmly locked the door and she glared at him angrily. Why did he have to come back now? One day she would be better. One day she would be able to see rain without thinking of the night in his arms. She tossed her coat on to a chair and walked away from him, trying to gain from distance what she could not achieve with her mind.

'My God! You're slim as a reed.'

'Don't you mean thin as a stick? I've had a virus.'

'I know.' He walked further into the room, looking round appreciatively. 'I've been to the studio. Ray pointed me in this direction. Paula gave me a coffee and a sackful of information. Your father greeted me with polite suspicion.'

'I was at the studio.' She had walked back through the park, hoping that the cold air would blow away her misery, but it hadn't helped at all and now he was here, looking at her with those dark, intense eyes.

'You'd just left. I missed you by seconds, but no matter. I've caught up with you now.'

'To no purpose. I can't think what you want.' She turned away, walking to the window and looking out at the fitful gusts of wind. 'No doubt you got all the information you needed from Paula.'

'Some of it. She told me about your illness, that you had left Westwind. She also told me that Bradshaw had left because of you.'

'I decline to take the blame,' Natalie said tightly, shaking with anguish at what Paula had rushed to tell him.

'Who's blaming you? Your father thought you were pregnant.'

'I wish I had been!' The words just seemed to burst out by themselves, private dreams she had nursed before she had known it was a false hope.

He was behind her without having seemed to have moved at all, his fingers parting her dark hair from her neck, his lips brushing her nape.

'Do you? Do you want my babies so badly, Natalie?'

'I didn't mean... I never meant...' Desire rushed through her like a tidal wave, defeating her. She was panic-stricken at her own folly but he pulled her back against him, holding her unyielding body against his warmth.

'I hope you did,' he said quietly, his voice low and dark, 'because no other woman is ever going to have my children.'

'Don't talk to me! I don't even want to hear your voice.' She was desolate, caught once again in his spell—and so easily.

'Because it bothers you?'

'You say words you don't mean. Unbelievable.' Her own voice was choking, trembling because she had lost all control of her feelings. His power was sweeping into her, slowly and surely as the hands moulded her fragile shoulders.

'I said I would follow you across the world and here I am.'

'Why? Why?' she asked brokenly.

'Because I love you. Because you're mine. Send me away and I'll just come back. I'm that sort of person.'

'You let me go. You just let me go. You thought that Neil...' She spun round to face him, tears on her cheeks, and he locked her against him with no hope of escape, his strong arms a circle around her waist.

'Surely you've heard of jealousy? It's the gut-wrenching feeling you get when you see somebody with the woman you love. I had to go away and cool off.'

'And what about that woman? Annette. You told her about us. You told her everything about the night that——'

His eyes darkened to anger and his grip on her waist tightened to near pain. 'Like hell I did!'

'So how did she know?'

He shrugged angrily. 'A shot in the dark that paid off because a green-eyed little witch was too unsure of me to think straight.' It was her fault again. She could see that clearly and he found himself facing that green blaze of temper he had seen when he had first met her, and so many times since.

'And what about all those other women?'

His lips quirked at her stormy insistence and it made her more angry than ever. She moved fretfully but he merely tightened his already punishing grip.

'What other women, my silly love? I've worked too damned hard all my life to be cast as Casanova. The only woman who has taken more than a few hours of my time has been my tempestuous sister, who is now firmly under Kane's thumb. The only woman I want is you.'

Natalie was still not appeased. Weeks of misery could not be simply pushed aside like that.

'You let me go,' she said flatly, the fire dying out of her suddenly. 'And you can let me go now. You're hurting me.'

'Then let's try another arrangement.' He swept her up into his arms, frowning as he felt her loss of weight. Before she could protest he was sitting on the settee, Natalie securely held in his lap. 'This is something we haven't done before,' he said with every appearance of satisfaction. 'We'll have to practise it until we get it off perfectly.'

Now she had no desire to move away. His hand was stroking her back and those dark eyes were looking into hers with such possession that she felt her whole tight little world begin to melt and disintegrate. He hadn't kissed her and he looked as if he had no thought to do it either.

Tears formed at the back of her eyes and she looked up at him mournfully.

'Why didn't you come when I left? You knew when I was going.'

'Why didn't you come to me? You knew where I was,' he countered, and she began to struggle fiercely, angry and frustrated.

'It's my fault! I know! It's *always* my fault!'

'Shh.' He held her still, pressing her head to his shoulder. 'I'll not tease you again, my sweetest Natalie. Kane told me something I had to have a good think about. He wants me in Venezuela, like yesterday. Sometimes I get into places where a woman would be endangered and I already know your ability to get into scrapes. Plenty of women go out to the sites, even when it's bad, but not my woman. I wanted to see it before I decided.'

'Decided what?' She was almost holding her breath, gazing up at him with wide eyes, and he smiled down at her, his lips brushing hers for the first time, just lightly.

'Decided to tell Kane to get himself another hatchet-man. You see, I'm getting married and my woman is a delicate butterfly who has to be treated very carefully. She's got a wild temper and a nasty way of blaming me for everything but all the same——'

He didn't finish because Natalie took matters into her own hands and reached up to him, winding her arms around his neck and pressing her lips to his.

'I love you,' she whispered fervently, and he tightened her against him, crushing her.

'I know,' he breathed into her mouth. 'How do you fancy Venezuela?'

'I'll go anywhere you go.' She could say no more because he caught her up more tightly still and covered her mouth with his, kissing her so hungrily that the whole world seemed to whirl away like the spinning autumn leaves outside.

'You can stop working,' he said firmly when she lay back against him, flushed and breathless. 'I can think of plenty of things to keep you busy.'

'Wrong again, so wrong,' Natalie said happily, looking up into the eyes that smiled down at her. 'I may have deserted my own dear father but I'm not stopping work. I've got books to write, plenty of them. I've got a crateful of notes and bundles of photographs. All I need is a typewriter and plenty of paper.'

'Maybe we'd better go by sea,' Kip mused thought-fully. 'Of course you could always have my baggage allowance. I expect I can manage with just one clean shirt.'

'Nothing matters if we're together,' Natalie said softly, her face filled with happiness. It was all too new, too wonderful, and she trembled even now in the strong arms that held her.

'It would have been pretty tricky with you at one side of the world and me at the other,' Kip pointed out, and she looked up at him quickly.

'Is that why you mentioned it? Why, we hardly knew each other. Surely you weren't thinking then...?'

'I don't waste time thinking about things like that, my green-eyed angel. I make plans. As for not knowing each other, the moment I set eyes on you I knew you were mine. You might not have been my idea of a television trouble-shooter but you were my idea of a woman—my woman.'

'I'll have to take you to meet my father properly,' Natalie sighed happily. 'I've got to warn you, he's a bit odd.'

'Don't worry, I've got two oddities in my family. Andrea and Aunt Maureen are planning the wedding.'

'Did you tell them?'

He laughed and shook his head, his teeth white against his tanned face.

'I decided to tell you first but Andrea had summed up the situation and informed Aunt Maureen. My sister is inclined to be a trifle bossy.'

'She's incredibly beautiful.' Natalie sighed and he kissed her smooth cheek, his hand stroking her breast until she arched against him.

'Is she? I didn't notice. All I seem to see is you, your witch-black hair, your green eyes. I've been in love with you since I first saw you and it's going to last more than a lifetime.'

She wanted to snuggle against him but he turned up her face, his restraint gone, claiming her mouth with such hungry passion that every other thought left her mind. She smiled against his lips and he felt it, his fair head lifting as he looked down at her.

'What is it, my love?'

'It's the rain bird,' she said dreamily. 'I never seem to stop hearing it. These weeks you've been away it's haunted my dreams. I wanted you so much and each night I could hear the song, see the green after the rain, feel your arms around me. The most wonderful night of my life.'

'There'll be other wonderful nights, darling,' he said huskily, looking down into her enchanted face, 'and days. Nothing will ever keep us apart again.'

He stood and lifted her, cradling her against him as if she was a precious delight.

'I'm going to love you,' he said thickly. 'I'm going to love you until the sad little look leaves your eyes and the smile comes back forever. You're mine, my beautiful Natalie, and nothing will keep us apart.'

Later in his arms she felt the worshipping warmth of his love and tears of happiness filled her eyes as in her head, clear and silvery sweet, she heard the song of the rain bird, a song of joy and love.

**Relive the romance...
Harlequin and Silhouette
are proud to present**

A program of collections of three complete novels by the most
requested authors with the most requested themes. Be sure to
look for one volume each month with three complete novels by
top name authors.

In June: **NINE MONTHS** Penny Jordan
                            Stella Cameron
                            Janice Kaiser

**Three women pregnant and alone. But a lot can
happen in nine months!**

In July: **DADDY'S
           HOME**   Kristin James
                            Naomi Horton
                            Mary Lynn Baxter

**Daddy's Home... and his presence is long
overdue!**

In August: **FORGOTTEN
           PAST**   Barbara Kaye
                            Pamela Browning
                            Nancy Martin

**Do you dare to create a future if you've forgotten
the past?**

Available at your favorite retail outlet.

HARLEQUIN®   *Silhouette*